THE GIRL'S GUIDE

TO

Vampires

All you need to know
about the original
BAD BOYS

BARB KARG

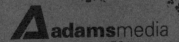
adamsmedia

AVON, MASSACHUSETTS

Published by
Adams Media, a division of F+W Media, Inc.
57 Littlefield Street, Avon, MA 02322. U.S.A.
www.adamsmedia.com

ISBN-10: 1-60550-819-5
ISBN-13: 978-1-60550-819-1

Printed in Canada.

J I H G F E D C B A

Library of Congress Cataloging-in-Publication Data
is available from the publisher.

This publication is designed to provide accurate and authoritative information with regard to the subject matter covered. It is sold with
the understanding that the publisher is not engaged in rendering legal, accounting, or other professional advice. If legal advice or other
expert assistance is required, the services of a competent professional
person should be sought.

—From a *Declaration of Principles* jointly adopted by a Committee
of the American Bar Association and a Committee of Publishers and
Associations

Many of the designations used by manufacturers and sellers to distinguish their product are claimed as trademarks. Where those designations appear in this book and Adams Media was aware of a trademark
claim, the designations have been printed with initial capital letters.

This book is available at quantity discounts for bulk purchases.
For information, please call 1-800-289-0963.

For Piper Maru. Our life. Our love. Our eternal light.

And for Anne Rice. For her eloquence, her incredible life's work, and her belief that in the darkness and light of life there remain shadows that call to us, beckoning that we may better understand that within the preternatural unknown there is much worth knowing.

Acknowledgments

Let it be said, that with all publications that require intense historical study and research, this is most definitely *not* a singular pursuit. When the subject is one that requires delving into a creature built more of legend than reality, that pursuit becomes that much trickier. To that end, there are many individuals I'd like to thank for their gracious aid in pursuing a bitingly dark subject with a light-heartedness for which I am eternally grateful.

For starters, I'd like to thank Adams Media for their support and encouragement, especially editor extraordinaire Lisa Laing, whose wit and exceptional professionalism I've greatly admired for all the years we've worked together; and director of innovation and epitome of class, Paula Munier, whom I love more than Cabernet *and* chocolate. I'd also like to thank copy chief Casey Ebert, and layout artist and designer Elisabeth Lariviere, for their swift and smart handling of *The Girl's Guide to Vampires.*

Most importantly, I am, as always, indebted to my family: George and Trudi Karg, Chris, Glen, Ethan, and Brady; and above all to my partner Rick Sutherland who is both my partner in crime and the love of my life. Likewise, I'm forever endeared to our close circle of friends and compadres, Ellen and Jim Weider, Jeans and Jim and the entire Spaite family, Jim V., the Scribe Tribe, Becca, J.R., and Gorgeous Sue, Doc Bauman, Mary, Jamie, and Michele and the gang who take such wonderful care of us and our kids, Richard Fox and his merry gang, and our beloved Blonde Bombshell. I'd like to give a special shout to my soul sister Antje Harrod for all of the amazing and diligent research she did for the book. Heart and soul, medear, you are the absolute best! And lest I forget, the lights of our lives, Sasha, Harley, Mog, Jinks, Maya, Scout, Bug, and especially Jazz and Piper. I thank you all. I adore you all. I love you with all my heart.

Contents

Introduction

Welcome, ladies, to *The Girl's Guide to Vampires*, chock full of everything you need to know about these quintessential creatures of the night! No doubt, you have many questions about vampires. How are they created? How have they evolved? Do they *really* transform into bats? Who is it that dreamed up Dracula in the first place? And most importantly, what's up with the cape and the fangs? Well, I'm happy to say that these important issues and many more are addressed in this snappy little book, which is sure to keep you mesmerized and glued to the edge of your coffin.

Did you know that over the centuries there have been multiple incarnations of vampires as documented in legend, folklore, fiction and nonfiction, movies, and alleged firsthand accounts of sightings and interactions? It's true, and they range from the creepy Greek *vrykolokas*, to Bram Stoker's *Dracula* to Christopher Lee's Hammer films to the notorious case of London's alleged Highgate Vampire, and a huge crypt overflowing with literature and film devoted entirely to naughty night stalkers.

Now it must be said, when it comes to vampires, you'll find a wide range of stories that in some cases have taken on lives of their own. As with all things dubbed paranormal, this is natural. For the purposes of this guide, I cover a wide variety of vampires from the traditional "I vant to suck your blood" ghoul to the romantic drawing-room bloodsucker to accounts of "real" vampires and pop-culture hotties such as *Twilight's* Edward Cullen. And make no mistake—we can't resist these immortal bad boys because we *all* give in to our wild rebellious side from time to time and the knowledge that what's good for us must be discovered by learning about what we *know* is bad for us!

By and large, the vampire, perhaps more so than any other legendary character, has been fictionalized and romanticized so much that it's almost overwhelming. But along the way, many diligent researchers, writers, historians, scholars, scientists, vampirologists, and folklorists have tackled the subject and presented a character full of history, mystery, romance—and major attitude. That said, for the majority of folks, vampires and vampirism is nothing more than the stuff of legends. However, as with mysterious figures such as Bigfoot and the Loch Ness Monster, there remains the possibility that if something hasn't been clearly disproven, there *is* the possibility that it can indeed exist. Don't you think?

Vampire legend and its eternal context is made up of an exceptional kaleidoscope of history, lore, and social commentary. All of that is what I seek to expose and introduce to you so that you may have a well-rounded initiation into a world filled with light, dark, and a huge gray area. Armed with this information, you alone can decide if creatures of the night do indeed walk among us, watching and waiting and perhaps even hoping that we gain a new understanding of why they hunt, how they live, and how they survive—whether in real life or purely in our minds. They are, and shall forever be known as, the ultimate immortal bad boys. They shock. They seduce. They frighten. And on occasion they even make us laugh. But be warned. If one thing holds true when it comes to all things vampire— their bite *is* worse than their bark. So start channeling your inner Buffy and get ready to uncover the world of the most famous undead creature in history.

Enjoy the ride!

Chapter 1

VAMPS AND SCAMPS: BLOODSUCKERS THROUGH THE AGES

As one of the most famous creatures in horror history, the vampire has experienced an evolution that few creatures built of lore, legend, and film have enjoyed. Do they really exist, or are they just a figment of our imaginations? From dusk till dawn, the dark belongs to the ultimate immortal bad boy, but as you'll learn, they see much more than their preternatural vision allows and endure a remnant of humanity that belies their bloodlust. It's time for you to grab your garlic, your crucifix, and your wits as you venture into the unpredictable and undead realm of the vampire.

Dancing in the Dark

It's the night of the homecoming dance, and as you approach the gym, you hear music permeating the cold night air. It's Rihanna's song "Umbrella," and as you move closer, the lyrics spill out into the night: *"When the sun shines, we'll shine together. Told you I'll be here forever."* Once inside the elaborately decorated gym, you soak in the commingling of laughter and bodies moving to the music. Standing amid a group of excited friends, you suddenly feel as if someone is watching you.

You gaze around, moving from face to face, searching for a connection, until at last you focus on a dark corner of the room. You shift your attention to your friends, but suddenly the fine hairs on the back of your neck stand on end and you feel a sudden chill. Your gaze returns to the dark corner. Is someone or some*thing* there? You squint, hoping to catch a better look. Distracted by the blaring music you turn away for a split-second before fixating again on the empty corner. This time you see a distinct shadow, one that moves slowly forward as if emerging from a dense fog.

In an instant, the shadow takes the form of a tall, ripped young man. The softness of his lustrous dark hair, which settles in waves just below his collar, stands in contrast to his eyes, which seem almost luminescent in their unblinking gaze. A couple crosses your path and your view is momentarily interrupted. You push past them and stare at the mysterious, gorgeous boy.

He's gone.

Your eyes dart around the room to no avail, but as you turn around, you find he's now standing next to you, his violet eyes locked in an intense stare and his lips parted in a sweet but wry smile. The music slows, and without a word, he takes your hand in his and leads you to the dance floor. His hand is cool to the touch, his lips quite rosy, and his face, a bit disguised under the cascading kaleidoscope of colored lights, appears to be of a very pale complexion.

He pulls you close in a gentle embrace as you sway to the melody, the notes diminishing to a slight lull in the background. He draws you closer and you feel the whisper of his breath upon your neck. You close your eyes, and as you do, your mind is flooded with strange thoughts and images. Who *is* this guy? Why have I never noticed him before? Why do I feel so safe and calm? You hear a deep inhalation, as the vein in your neck throbs. When you open your eyes, you're alone on the dance floor.

You've just had your first encounter with a vampire.

If Looks Could Kill

If you really did meet a vampire, how would you react? Would you be excited? Terrified? Ecstatic? Or would you be really curious about how they came to be a bloodsucker and anxious to hear of their centuries-long adventures? Very likely it's all of the above, with the added measure of wanting to learn all about their legendary superpowers and what it would be like to live forever. After all, who wouldn't want to know a few immortal secrets—especially when told by a drop-dead (or undead) dreamboat. But before you get all sweet and sweaty over the ultimate romantic rogue, one with looks that can—quite literally—kill, you need to get a strong sense of who, or what, you're dealing with.

When you hear the word *vampire*, what's the first thing that comes to mind? Is it the gorgeous hottie you've just danced with, or is it a gaunt, menacing gent with a hypnotic stare, who's clothed in a fine black tuxedo enveloped by an exquisite opera cloak?

If it's the latter, then you've no doubt been influenced by Bela Lugosi in the 1931 classic film *Dracula*, who gives us the perfect representation of the traditional *drawing-room vampire*—one so deceptively aristocratic that he melds perfectly into respectable society.

The truth is, vampires comes in all shapes and sizes and all measure of physical appearance, from hunk to gruesome fiend to supermodel glamour gal. For the majority of us, the word *vampire* conjures up a bloodthirsty monster who's looking to make you his midnight snack. While that may be true for many vampires throughout history, it isn't always the case. Some immortal bad boys and girls are romantic heroes, some are searching for a cure to their affliction, and some want desperately to be accepted by society.

To truly understand vampires it's necessary to examine the quintessential triad of the vampire realm: folklore, *Dracula* author Bram Stoker and his precursors, and film. It is from that trio that all of the vampires as we know them today have spawned—from Count Dracula to Count Duckula and beyond. The vampire legend truly *is* immortal and as you'll learn within the pages of this guide, there's no ending to the travails of history's most entrancing blood-obsessed bad boy. The study of vampires, however, immediately elicits a coffin full of questions. How are they created? How do they survive? What kind of powers do they have? How can they be destroyed? Would I *really* want to be a vampire?

Undead and Underfed

If vampires are your fangtastic obsession, then you're in for a fascinating and fiendish rollercoaster ride that will take you from ancient times to the present day. For example, did you know that Dracula isn't the first vampire to plague the living? Indeed not. What you might find surprising is that vampires have been part of folklore for centuries and have taken the form of all types of creatures who rise from the grave and wreak havoc on the living. In many ways these creepy stories helped craft the vampire legends and lore as we know them today.

By definition, as conceived in folklore (particularly in Europe), a *vampire* is a reanimated corpse, or *revenant*, who rises from the grave to partake of the blood or flesh of the living through the use of elongated canine teeth. They are *preternatural*, indicating something beyond what is natural or normal. That said, the vampiric creatures of lore are decidedly *not* the debonair likes of Christopher Lee or Edward Cullen nor the lavish and exquisite vampires of Anne Rice's imaginings. No, these hideous corpses are more in keeping with *Night of the Living Dead* than *Love at First Bite*. Take heed of that warning, as you'll now be introduced to the first bloodsuckers through fascinating ancient legends from all over the world. In the same vein, you'll also learn about a few famous "real-life" bad boys whose wickedly wild antics are sure to keep your blood pumping.

European Bloodsuckers

There's little question that the vampire we've come to revere in entertainment and fear in reality wouldn't exist without the lurid tales of life-sucking demons throughout Europe. Although independence from world powers and influence was a cornerstone of the birth of America as an international power, as a people we're still inextricably linked to European cultures through history and heritage. The vampire of Europe is the forefather of the vampiric mythologies we embrace, and the basis for virtually all film and fictional forays into the world of the undead.

> Unlike seductive and dashingly debonair bloodsuckers, or the sultry, vixenish vamps of popular culture, the blood drinker of European lore was invariably hideously ugly and foul smelling, and absolutely the *last* creature on earth you'd want passionately nibbling your neck in the middle of the night.

Let's face it. These critters are reanimated corpses with vampiric tendencies. Definitely *not* the kind of boy you'd take home to meet Mom and Dad! While tales of horrific nightcrawlers permeated nearly all of Europe, it was Eastern Europe that gave birth to the lore that has evolved into the mythology of modern society. So, buckle up and prepare yourself for the vampires of European lore, beginning with the fascinating fiends of Greece.

Going Greek!

While you may be familiar with the mythological gods of ancient Greece, you might not know that according to legend, it was those same all-powerful deities who bred the creatures who would become the ancestors of vampires throughout the folklore of European history. The origination of vampiric demons in ancient Greece began in the world of the supernatural and remained there for centuries. Not surprising to vampire aficionados, it was Zeus, the supreme god of Greek mythology, who would become responsible for the creation of one of the earliest life-sucking demons in history—and he did it with an all-too-mortal bit of hanky-panky with another woman.

THE LEGENDARY LAMIA

The writings and legends of ancient Greeks, including references from Aristophanes and Aristotle, tell the tale of an illicit love affair between the omnipotent Zeus and the Libyan princess Lamia, who's variously described as the daughter of the sea god Poseidon or a daughter of Poseidon's son, Belus. The downside of this celestial fling is that it attracted the wrath of Hera, Zeus' jealous wife, who took vengeance upon the unfortunate Lamia by kidnapping and killing all of her god-spawned children and driving the bereft woman into exile.

Grief-stricken and unable to retaliate against the power of the gods who'd brought her such misery, Lamia began a campaign of exacting revenge upon humankind by stealing and sucking the life from the babies of mortal mothers. In later legendary incarnations, Lamia evolved into a legion of unearthly beings with the upper bodies of women and the lower shapes of serpents. These creatures are called *lamiai*, and they suck the blood of children and can also alter their appearance at will to seduce young men and lead them to ruin or death. Hell hath no fury like a woman scorned!

GETTING VAMPY WITH THE *VRYKOLAKAS*

In Greece, the most ancient of the demons with vampiric tendencies are directly tied to the supernatural world of spirits sired by the gods, but soon after Greece's conversion to Christianity, there grew the cultural suspicion that demons and the recently deceased were often one and the same. In modern terms, the dead who return to life are revenants, and in Greece, they're known as *vrykolakas*. Although there are various spellings of the term and variations of the word itself throughout regions of Greece, the vrykolakas are generally considered to be the most virulent demons of the undead, who return to life to cause misery to the living. Although the Greek interpretation of vrykolakas was essentially vampiric in nature, variations of the same term were used by the Slavs to describe the equally frightful *lycanthropes* or *lycans*, otherwise known as *werewolves*.

SLAVIC VAMPIRES

The importance of the earliest Greek references to vampiric creatures is often understated, but the Greeks gave us much of the first written reports of such unholy beings, with accounts dating back as far as the first century. As with the vrykolakas, the Slavic influence is crucial to the development of Greek vampire legends, and although the early Slavs weren't known for creating a rich written history, they would certainly become the bearers of lore that would eventually creep into Western Europe, and into our worst nightmares.

For example, according to one report from the early 1700s, the people in a Bohemian village in what's now the Czech Republic drove a stake into the corpse of a suspected *upir*. The hideous creature merely laughed and thanked them for giving him a stick to fight off pesky dogs! The startled villagers quickly solved their vampiric dilemma by burning the corpse. Suffice to say, the Slavic people—from the Slavic countries, including Slovakia, the Czech Republic, Belarus, Russia,

Ukraine, Bosnia, Bulgaria, Croatia, Montenegro, and Serbia—created vampiric legends that would later multiply and spread like wildfire.

Here are a few of the most popular troublesome bloodsucking creatures:

- **The *Upir***: The mainstay of rural Slovakian and Czech vampire folklore, the upir is the revived and rotting corpse of the recently deceased. It's thought to have two hearts and two souls, and will suck the blood from its victims, often suffocating them with a crushing embrace. What's worse, the upir can not only spread deadly disease, but can kill with a glance from its evil eye. Who knew that looks really can kill?

- **The Bulgarian *Vampir***: A deceased human who returns to life from the grave, maintaining every physical evidence of its former existence as a perfectly healthy human. Vampirs can safely move to areas where they weren't known in life and live a seemingly anonymous but normal existence by day, and create havoc with the living by night. Suffice to say that vampirs are sneaky little monsters!

- **The *Ustrel***: A nasty little vampire created from the souls of children born on a Saturday, but who pass away before being baptized. It's believed that the ustrel, in the invisible form of a spirit, can claw its way out of the grave to drain the blood from livestock, and hide behind the horns or hind legs of its prey.

- **The Bosnian *Lampir***: The lampir is thought primarily to be responsible for epidemics, and crawls from its grave as a hideously rotting and disease-ridden corpse for the sole purpose of infecting and bringing grief to those who subsequently succumb to and die of disease.

- **The Russian *Uppyr***: The decaying, reanimated remains of the dead who refuse to stay buried, the uppyr's undead state is closely linked to behavior that runs counter to religious piousness. Virtually anyone who strays outside the teachings of the Russian Orthodox Church is a prime candidate for becoming an uppyr.

ROMANIAN ROGUES

Although Slavic folklore can be generally credited with the initial development of vampires as the source of virtually every natural calamity that could fall upon a society in the first millennia in Eastern Europe, the Slavs also greatly influenced the legends of their non-Slavic neighbors.

Of these, Romania is unquestionably the most well known and is inextricably linked to the lore of vampirism in Europe, primarily as a result of Bram Stoker's *Dracula* and the light his 1897 novel cast on the often horrific activities of Dracula's alleged real-life inspirational genesis, Romania's Vlad the Impaler (see Chapter 2). Although Romania has throughout the centuries been bordered by the Slavic regions of what are now Bulgaria, Serbia, and the Ukraine, many of Romania's earliest political and social ties were with its Hungarian neighbors to the west.

Despite this amalgam of political and cultural sway, Romania has historically maintained its association with the ancient Roman Empire—which is the very namesake of Romania. It also has a host of creepy vampiric creatures.

THE STRIGOI

Despite the influences of Slavic vampire legend, the lore of vampires in Romania has maintained its own distinction in terminology and practice. In the Romanian principality of Transylvania—homeland of the legendary Vlad Dracula and the fictional Count Dracula—vampirism actually pulls double duty with both an inconspicuous living vampire, *strigoi vii*; and a dead vampire, the *strigoi mort*, thought to leave its tomb and take the form of an animal to haunt and harass the living.

The term *strigoi* (also spelled *strigoii*) is taken from the word *striga*, or witch, and describes entities who are doomed to become vampires after death. In legend, the association between witches and vampires is clear, with the strigoi vii and strigoi mort believed to gather at night to plot against the living. The strigoi mort are the deadliest of the Romanian vampires, and

9

will return from the grave to suck the life blood of their families and livestock, before eventually moving on to attack neighbors in their village.

> In Francis Ford Coppola's 1992 blockbuster *Bram Stoker's Dracula*, Gary Oldman as Prince Vlad in his youthful incarnation pays homage to Romanian lore in his first encounter with Mina Murray (Winona Ryder) in London. At a viewing of the Cinematograph, a white wolf wreaks havoc in the crowd. When it corners Mina, Vlad subdues the wolf by yelling "Strigoi!"

THE ALBANIAN SHTRIGA

Just as legends of Romanian vampirism take many of their cues from Slavic folklore, the southeastern European nation of Albania has also adopted a similar approach to the undead. As with Romania, the Albanian *shtriga* possesses witch-like characteristics. The term *shtriga*, which evolves from the Latin *strix*, or owl, describes a demonic flying creature of the night. The shtriga is believed to be a witch who behaves normally during daylight hours, but who at night will transform into an airborne insect, such as a fly or moth, and attack victims to drink their blood. In case of a shtriga attack, be sure to have your bug zapper fired up and at the ready!

WATCH YOUR BACK!

The vampires of Germany, as with other European bloodsuckers, owe their heritage to the Slavic vampires of Eastern Europe largely because of Slavic incursions into eastern Germany in the tenth century. The best-known incarnation of vampires in northern Germany are the *nachtzeherer,* or night wastes, who return from the dead after gnawing on their own extremities and clothing, presenting a hideous *Night of the Living Dead* image of partially eaten hands and arms to the living who happen across them.

And just so you're fully prepared, here are a few more European creatures to be on the lookout for:

- **The *Alp*:** Typically a sorcerer capable of assuming the form of a bird or cat in order to work its mischief. Alps enter the thoughts of sleeping victims and create nightmares, often resulting in convulsions and fits of hysteria. A common sign of a midnight alp attack is awakening with a sudden, crushing pressure on one's chest and an intense feeling of being suffocated.
- **The *Schrattl*:** A variation of the Germanic alp, the schrattl is a vampire born of a human corpse that has eaten away at its funerary shroud and risen from the grave. Schrattl attack their families and livestock first, and then move on to harass the rest of the community, often driving their victims to insanity. On occasion, they're also held responsible for diseases.
- ***Woodwives*:** Posing as benign fairies, woodwives attack hunters and woodcutters who venture deep into the woods. Deceased forest wanderers who were sometimes found near trails leading into the deep woods were generally assumed to be victims of woodwives who'd taken offense at their incursions. Suffice to say that woodwives are *not* Tinkerbell!
- **The *Baobban Sith*:** Seductive maidens who can take on the appearance of crows and ravens to move freely about. They lure travelers and hunters into singing and dancing with them, and during the course of the merriment slay them. Clearly Baobban Sith's are the ultimate party poopers.
- **The Welsh *Hag*:** A female demon who can take on the forms of a young maiden, a mature matron, or an ugly old crone. The old crone is the most feared because she signifies impending death and ruin, and is generally seen as the symbol of a washerwoman who rinses blood-soaked clothing in streams.
- **The *Gwrach y Rhibyn*:** Another form of hideously aged woman who can be seen at crossroads threatening travelers, or who's seen only in brief glimpses beside streams and ponds.

Latin American Suckers

Independent of the Slavic vampire traditions, the countries of what are now Latin America have developed their own distinctive vampire legends. The Aztec and Mayan civilizations, which ruled much of what is now Central America and Mexico, have a history of bloodthirsty deities that predate the first Spanish explorers, and their influence is still felt in modern lore, particularly in rural areas. Here are a few of these legendary critters:

- **The *Camazotz*:** In Mayan lore, the Camazotz is a deity with a human male body and the head of a bat, and may have developed its origins from the vampire bats of South America. The Camazotz personifies death and sacrifice, and people greatly fear the caves that are thought to be his lair.
- ***Cihuateteo*:** Deities of the souls of women who die in childbirth, the cihuateteo give strength to warriors in battle. Their physical remains wander the earth to spread disease and madness. Food offerings to appease them are often left at crossroads where the creatures are thought to gather and from where they launch their nighttime assaults on the living.
- ***Tlahuelpuchi*:** A bloodsucking witch who can transform into a variety of animals in order to roam about freely. These creatures are particularly mean-spirited. Garlic, onions, and metal can be placed in or around a baby's crib for protection from this fiendish vampire witch, but unexplained infant deaths to this day are still often attributed to the tlahuelpuchi in remote areas of Mexico.
- **The *Chupacabra*:** Since the 1990s, bloody attacks on livestock in Puerto Rico, Mexico, Texas, and as far north as Maine have been attributed to the elusive chupacabra (which means "goat sucker"), and have triggered media hysterics and a handful of fanciful horror films and appearances on serial television dramas such as The *X-Files*. The few alleged chupacabras killed by wary ranchers have turned out to be ill, emaciated, and mange-ridden coyotes. Where's Fox Mulder when you need him?

Indian and Far Eastern Fangsters

Although vampires as we've come to love and loathe them in western culture, literature, and film are invariably of European descent, the power, fear, and fascination of vampiric fright knows no borders. What you may find interesting is that many vampire experts, also called vampirologists, believe India may well have been an original source of some vampire mystique.

Throughout the millennia, Indian culture and religion has generated an enormous variety of deities, demons, and superstitious beliefs and legends, and many of the ancient vampire-like Indian entities are still alive and well in modern lore. Here are a few of the bloodthirsty creatures of Indian and Asian lore:

- **The Chinese *Jiang Shi*:** Often referred to as the hopping ghost, the jiang shi (also spelled *chiang shih*) is the reanimated corpse of a victim of drowning, hanging, suicide, or smothering. The universally vampiric garlic remedy is effective against this nasty creature, as are salt and metal filings. And curiously, the sound of thunder is a natural killer of the beasts, so next time you're being chased by one . . . make sure it's during a thunderstorm!

- **The Japanese *Kappa*:** A creepy critter resembling a hairless monkey with large round eyes and webbed fingers and toes, the kappa springs from its hiding places in waterways and ponds, and has the distasteful habit of sucking blood from its victims through their intestines. Gross!

- *Langsuyar* **and** *Pontianak*: In Malaysia, a pair of vampires can spring from the bodies of a mother who dies in childbirth, as well as that of her stillborn baby. The mother becomes a langsuyar, and the child reappears as a pontianak, and both reanimate to seek jealous revenge on living victims, showcasing the unnerving habit of ripping open their bellies to suck out blood.

- **The Indonesian *Penanggala*:** Often described as a midwife who has made a pact with the devil, the penanggala is normal by day, but by night becomes a detached head with a tail of entrails and intestines dangling from her severed neck. She hunts for women in labor and perches on rooftops to wail during a victim's childbirth and attempts to lap the blood of a mother and newborn with a long, thin tongue.

- **Indian *Rakshasas*:** Fanged ogres in human form, rakshasas inhabit cemeteries, from where they wander into the night to attack infants and pregnant women. The *hatu-dhana* (also spelled *yatu-dhan*), are an evolutionary step below the rakshasas and are believed to feed on human remains left by a rakshasa.
- **Indian *Bhutas*:** Spirits of the those who are insane, who were killed by sudden, accidental death, or who suffer physical defects, the bhuta inhabit ruins and cremation sites, and can enter the bodies of victims to feed on corpses and even the living. They're also held responsible for droughts, crop failures, illness, and insanity—or for that matter, virtually any calamity. So if your Gameboy goes missing . . . blame it on a bhuta!
- **Indian *Vetala*:** The vetala, also known as a *betail*, is another demonic creature that co-opts the bodies of living victims, and like many of the Indian night stalkers, delights in causing miscarriages, and driving people mad.

Dead and Loving It

Now that you've learned about the creepy-crawly vampires of folklore, it's time to explore a pair of real-life bloodsuckers. Bear in mind that throughout the centuries there have been numerous accounts of alleged encounters with vampires, and while the majority are the stuff legends are made of, there are a few well-documented incidents that have become legendary for their intrigue and even more so for the hysteria they caused. Peter Plogojowitz and Arnod Paole are two of those monsters, and as you'll see, they scared the knickers off everyone who heard of their exploits.

PETER, PETER, PEASANT BLEEDER

What's of particular interest in the case of Serbian peasant Peter Plogojowitz is that his sordid tale is actually quite well documented, despite having taken place in the Serbian village of Kisilova in 1725. As the story goes, Peter Plogojowitz, by rights an average man of little distinction, passed away and was buried in the Rahm district of Kisilova, Serbia. Just over a week later, a mysterious twenty-four hour illness, which some report as involving a loss of blood, struck nine villagers of varying ages resulting in their deaths.

Plogojowitz's wife claimed that her dearly departed husband had paid her a visit in order to collect his shoes (some accounts claim he visited his son for food on several occasions and when refusing dear old dead dad, the son died). This substantiated the reports—prior to their demise—from those who fell ill, that Plogojowitz not only visited them, but attempted to strangle them.

As is often done in these situations, Plogojowitz was exhumed to ascertain if he bore typical vampiric signs, including a lack of decomposition, a ruddy complexion, fingernails and hair showing growth, and the presence of fresh blood. With the cooperation of authorities and military personnel, the poor man was dug up, and according to accounts, did indeed bear the telltale signs of a vampire. Some of his skin had sloughed off to show new skin underneath, his hair and nails had grown, there was blood near his mouth, and he appeared relatively intact. It should come as no surprise that his appearance was cause for panic and anger.

The authority of the district and the clergyman who oversaw the exhumation were faced with villagers who took matters into their own hands—literally. Plogojowitz's corpse was staked through the heart, after which it was reported that fresh blood leaked from his chest and out the mouth and ears. The poor man's corpse was promptly set alight and burned to ash. Naturally, this gave cause for all of his alleged victims to also be exhumed and measures taken, such as garlic stuffed in their mouths, to make certain they would rest in peace.

One thing that you should know, which certainly comes into play with Peter Plogojowitz as well as many other alleged vampires such as Arnod Paole, is the subject of *decomposition*. By definition, decomposition is the decay of a dead body or any organic matter. Where folkloric vampires and other corpses were concerned, little was understood or surmised at the time that perhaps the bloating due to internal gases and buildup of fluids accounted for the frightening groans and spurting blood that a corpse emitted as it was being staked.

ARNOD'S AMAZING UNDEAD ADVENTURE

Two years after the Plogojowitz case came yet another incident that became even more famous, in part as a result of Austrian regimental field surgeon Johannes Flückinger's widely read report entitled *Visum et Repertum* (alternately translated as "Seen and Heard" or "Seen and Discovered"), which was published and presented to the Austrian Emperor in 1732. Flückinger's report, which states that vampires did indeed exist, focused on a Serbian vampire epidemic, and the initial vampire in this instance was alleged to be Serbian soldier Arnod Paole (also cited as Arnold Paul).

Though accounts vary, the story goes that in 1727, Paole returned home to the village of Medvegia (also spelled Meduegna) on the outskirts of Belgrade. It's said that Paole himself told of an encounter he'd had with a vampire while stationed in Greece, which was then known as Turkish Serbia (other accounts describe this incident as Paole having had a dream).

The *Repertum* states that Paole "had eaten from the earth of the vampire's grave and had smeared himself with the vampire's blood, in order to be free of the vexation he had suffered." Unfortunately for the former soldier, his "cure" proved futile, and he allegedly spread his tall tale around the village—a seemingly harmless endeavor that would prove to be his unearthly undoing.

STAKE OUT

Not long after arriving home, Paole died as a result of falling off a hay wagon. A month or so after his interment, local villagers made known that Arnod Paole was *not* going peacefully into that good night. He was, in fact, troubling them and was allegedly responsible for four killings.

As with Peter Plogojowitz, these accusations became grounds for digging up Paole to examine his corpse for signs of vampirism, which they did forty days *after* his burial. Again, the folkloric signs of the ultimate night stalker came into sharp focus. According to the *Repertum*, the villagers found that Paole was "quite complete and undecayed, and that fresh blood had flowed from his eyes, nose, mouth, and ears; that the shirt, the covering, and the coffin were completely bloody; that the old nails on his hands and feet, along with the skin, had fallen off, and that new ones had grown."

According to local custom, a stake was driven through Paole's heart and he "gave an audible groan and bled copiously." After he was done scaring everyone with his final death knell, he was burned to ashes.

THE MEDVEGIA VAMPIRES

Whereas the Plogojowitz case ended with his burning, Paole's did not. The panic his alleged vampirism caused and the resulting exhumation, observation, and destruction of the chain reaction of victims afflicted by vampirism gave those victims the dubious title of "The Medvegia Vampires."

The logic that ensued after Paole's destruction was such that the corpses of his four aforementioned victims were also dispatched. But it didn't stop there. Common assumption dictated that Paole fed upon local cattle, and given that villagers consumed their cattle, *they* were also infected and in danger of becoming bloodsuckers. The *Repertum* states that within three months, seventeen individuals perished within two or three days as a result of illness.

One even cited a fellow deceased villager as her attacker! Was it a coincidence? Not bloody likely. As one would expect, all of the unfortunate deceased were exhumed, and the results of Flückinger's report are highly detailed in regard to the status of each corpse's condition, similar in many ways to that of Paole, with various traits that modern science might attribute to typical decomposition—or not. The few who were simply decomposed were reburied; however, the majority of the Medvegia Vampires were summarily decapitated, burned, and their ashes released into the river.

From Here to Eternity

So what do you think? Are the vampires of lore and legend the type of fangtastic bad boys you'd like to hang with for all eternity? It's doubtful. But their history is crucial in understanding the evolution of vampires and vampirism in its widely differing incarnations. As a superstition, scientific or psychological study, and even as scapegoats, bloodthirsty nightcrawlers continue to be feared throughout the world, whether in our imaginations or in real life.

With that rich history, it's easy to see how writers of the day were inspired to create mesmerizing bloodsuckers who would capture public imagination, much like Anne Rice has accomplished with her legendary *Vampire Chronicles*, and like Stephenie Meyer and Charlaine Harris have done with their romantic and quirky blood drinkers (see Chapter 6). With that in mind, let's go batty and take a peek into the mausoleum of the first literary vampires who, with little remorse and plenty of finesse, continue to keep us mesmerized.

Chapter 2

Masters of Immortality

After learning about the fiendish folkloric vamps of ancient times, you're probably wondering how they evolved from creepy critters to the elegant, arrogant, and deceptive rogues of the modern day. The credit for that progression goes to the first literary vampires and several authors who brought the tall, dark, and deadly types out of the shadows and into our parlors. The most renowned of those mavericks is Bram Stoker, whose entire career can be summed up in a single word—Dracula. So grab your cape and your best set of fangs, because we're about to uncover the father of all immortal bad boys.

Early Writings of the Undead

Of all the prominent authors of celebrated fiction, Bram Stoker is probably the least well-known writer of one of the most famous stories in history. Ironic, isn't it? Stoker's frightening depiction of the quintessential vampire in his innovatively constructed 1897 masterpiece *Dracula* brought the world of the undead to life. His concept of the eternal battle of good versus evil has evolved and flourished into the foundation of literary and cinematic pursuits that have left us breathless, drained, and dying for more. What you might find particularly intriguing is that while Stoker and his characters are unquestionably the most famous, his vampiric tale wasn't the first to stake a claim in vampire evolution.

The Vampyre

There's a famous true-life story in literary history that's commonly attached to Mary Shelley's 1818 masterpiece *Frankenstein*, but most folks might not realize its significance to the world of vampire literature.

In May of 1816, English poet Lord Byron, his traveling companion and personal physician John Polidori, poet Percy Bysshe Shelley, and his future wife, Mary Wollstonecraft Godwin were gathered on the shores of Switzerland's Lake Geneva at the Villa Diodati. En route to Italy, stalled by bad weather, they passed the time by each of them concocting a ghost story to share with the others. Byron produced a partial tale about a vampire, Polidori told a story hinged on a "skull-headed lady," and eighteen-year-old Mary began the basis of *Frankenstein*, which along with *Dracula*, would become one of the most famous horror novels of all time.

In 1819, *The Vampyre: A Tale*, which Polidori penned using the framework of Byron's story as told at the Villa Diodati, was published in England's *The New Monthly Magazine*. The short story focuses on the treacherous bloodsucker Lord Ruthven, who by no small coincidence bears a striking resemblance to Lord Byron. This fact alone created what would come to be known as *Byronic vampires,* meaning those who possess characteristics typical of characters in Byron's body of work or his physical appearance. Some scholars speculate that Polidori's swiping of Byron's original idea was fueled in part by revenge for his Lordship's cruelty to Polidori.

What's highly significant about *The Vampyre* is not only its being recognized as the first true work of vampire fiction, but the character of Lord Ruthven. As a precursor to Dracula, Ruthven first displayed the sinister effects of vampirism and the predatory capacities of a creature who, unlike the typical folkloric vampire, is a handsome, self-possessed, evil aristocrat whose love of manipulation is rivaled only by his lust to kill.

> Ruthven is by all accounts a monster; a charming drawing-room aristocrat whose irresistibility and utter ruthlessness has been channeled throughout literature and film ever since. Ruthven's so-called Byronic features, the pallor of his skin, his bloodlust, seductiveness, arrogance, and all his preternatural manipulations would immediately inspire and incite mimicry in the vampiric literary realm.

VARNEY THE VAMPYRE

Though there were many representations of literary vampires spun off from Polidori's Lord Ruthven, it wasn't until the mid-1840s that the public was introduced to a different kind of vampire, one whose appearance and ferocity harkens back to the bloodsucking critters of folklore. Sir Francis Varney is the star of the penny dreadful (a cheap comic or storybook) turned novel *Varney the Vampyre or the Feast of Blood,* thought initially to be written by Thomas Preskett Prest, with the general consensus now being that its author is James Malcolm Rymer. Hideous in his conception, Sir Francis Varney (ambiguously cited as the reanimated corpse of 1640 suicide victim Marmaduke Bannerworth) is the epitome of cruelty and banality, his corpse-like form stalking young girls in a disjointed epic that ran as 109 separate publications and later as a novel with 220 chapters amounting to over 860 pages.

One of Varney's victims dramatically describes him by saying: "There was a tall, gaunt form—there was the faded ancient apparel—the lustrous metallic-looking eyes—its half-opened mouth, exhibiting tusk-like teeth! It was—yes, it was—the vampyre!" What Varney represents to vampire literature is yet another stage of evolution. Unlike Lord Ruthven, Varney draws from the dark side of folklore while also retaining the traditional characteristics that have become synonymous with the drawing-room vampire in general.

"CARMILLA"

In 1872, another fold of the cloak that would envelop the beginnings of vampire literature and cinema was revealed in the form of Irishman Joseph Sheridan Le Fanu's "Carmilla," a novella published as part of his collection of tales *In a Glass Darkly.*

What Le Fanu (often cited as J. Sheridan or simply Sheridan Le Fanu) pulled out of the vampiric crypt is no less critical than Polidori's contributions—some would argue even more so—as he not only brought the seductive vampire to the forefront—he made his antagonistic bloodsucker a woman!

> In the telling of "Carmilla," one can clearly see where Le Fanu was influenced by folkloric tales, in particular the process of staking, beheading, and burning a vampire, the condition of Carmilla in her grave, and her transformation into a cat.

As a demon and seductress, Carmilla has all the makings of a traditional vampire with the added distinction of bringing the female-obsessed vampire to the fore, a precedent that thereafter appears throughout the history of female vampires. She also carries over a host of vampiric traits. Like Lord Ruthven and Sir Francis Varney, Carmilla is invigorated by the moon, has fangs, endures a "quiet" sleep with alleged sleepwalking tendencies, can hypnotize, and has the ability to shape shift.

Carmilla Karnstein stands as one of the most influential literary and cinematic vampires in history, and her presence cannot be understated. Simply put, she's the mother of all female vampires. In crafting his spooky tale, Le Fanu, as did Polidori and Rymer and a handful of other writers of the day, gave us a glimpse of the world through preternatural eyes. But it wasn't until another Irishman submitted a novel originally called *The Undead*, that the figure of the drawing-room vampire become set in stone as a permanent fixture in the cryptic vampire realm.

Stoking the Flames

The great irony of Bram Stoker's phenomenally successful effort in creating his incredible and immortal character is that during his lifetime, he would never realize the impact *Dracula* would have on millions of mesmerized readers and moviegoers.

During much of his adult life, Stoker remained a relatively obscure figure who regularly brushed shoulders with the famous and near-famous, but it would only be after his death that he would gain distinction as the mastermind of one of the most celebrated characters in the world.

FORMULATING DRACULA

If you've read *Dracula*, then you're likely familiar with the story, in which affable solicitor Jonathan Harker is dispatched to Castle Dracula in Transylvania in order to conduct a London real estate transaction with Count Dracula. What results is Harker being imprisoned in the castle and, through a number of bizarre incidents and encounters, realizes his captor is a vampire.

Dracula travels to London on the ship *Demeter*, and once there inflicts his bite on wealthy free spirit Lucy Westenra, who's being courted by Arthur Holmwood, Quincey P. Morris, and Dr. Jack Seward. After Lucy becomes a vampire and is killed with the help of Abraham Van Helsing, Harker's fiancée

Mina Murray becomes Dracula's next best hope of securing eternal arm candy.

Much has been written and debated over the past century about the inspiration for the character of Count Dracula, and his horrific proclivities for drinking the blood of humanity. Although there's little doubt that Bram Stoker appropriated his villain's name from Prince Vlad Dracula of Wallachia, Romania, the physical characteristics of Dracula are commonly believed to have been inspired by legendary English actor and Stoker's business associate at the Lyceum Theatre, Henry Irving. The great actor's stature, grace, and facial features are found in Stoker's account of the literary Count, and it's probable that Irving's fiery temperament provided more than a little inspiration for Dracula's forbidding nature.

Of equal interest in Stoker's novel are the band of characters who play into Dracula's scheming, and who eventually prevail in bringing the epitome of evil to a deservedly ghastly end. Unlike the typical screeching, blood-spurting film vampire, Dracula simply crumbles to dust.

What Stoker can lay claim to is the fact that Count Dracula ultimately became synonymous with the word *vampire* in that his portrayal struck a chord in the collective conscious of society in Victorian England and eventually, the entire world.

Replete with drama, romance, graphic horror, supernatural occurrences, and punctuated by the underlying subtext of the repression of physical intimacy, the politics of the aristocracy bleeding the lower classes, and the ultimate religious fight of good versus evil, *Dracula* stands on its own as the most recreated and popular novel in history.

DEAR DIARY . . .

If you haven't read *Dracula*, it truly is a fascinating adventure. One of its more unique aspects, aside from the arrogance of its main character, is the format in which Stoker chose to tell the tale, relying on the literary device of presenting excerpts from the journals and diaries of his key players (excluding

Dracula), interspersed with other bits of crucial information such as letters, newspaper articles, phonograph recordings, and the like.

This gives the novel the distinct advantage of portraying fictional firsthand accounts of the drama and horror as it takes place in Transylvania and Victorian London. Stoker's legendary characters are arguably some of the most mimicked in cinematic history, each in their own right granted a distinctly human immortality. To understand where all the cute immortal bad boys come from, you need to know their "father" and the characters who are out to get him:

- **Count Dracula:** The father of all immortal bad boys, this relentless bloodsucker set the standard for many of the vampire's traits, including the ability to transform into a bat, a wolf, mist, and elemental dust; an aversion to mirrors, garlic, and holy artifacts; magnified senses, and sleeping upon native soil; to name a few.
- **Jonathan Harker:** One of the primary heroes of *Dracula*, young, handsome solicitor Harker is perhaps the best representation of the "perfect" English gentleman, one who's thrust into a situation beyond his imagining and forced to literally fight to the death to save his love and eventual wife, Mina Murray. Harker in many ways epitomizes the average man whose proper belief system and morals are challenged to the very brink of his sanity.
- **Abraham Van Helsing:** The Dutch professor, doctor, and philosopher turned vampire hunter is unquestionably the hero of *Dracula*. It is Van Helsing who discovers Dracula's strengths, weaknesses, and how to destroy him. Van Helsing versus Dracula is an epic battle, rife with spiritual, mental, physical, and metaphorical symbolism that set the precedent for all vampire stories to the present day.
- **Wilhemina "Mina" Murray:** Mina is the representation of all things good and moral in Victorian society, standing forth against the legacy of evil that so permeates Dracula. Pure and virtuous in her thinking and behavior, it's

ultimately this assistant school mistress who becomes the object of Dracula's obsession and with whom he shares his blood in an attempt to make her his bride.

- **Lucy Westenra:** A woman of wealth and frivolity who's courted by Arthur Holmwood, Dr. Seward, and Quincey P. Morris. Lucy provides opposition to Mina in the metaphorical sense, as Lucy is the "bad" girl who becomes a vampire by Dracula's bite and turns to the dark side. Trapped by Van Helsing, she's staked by Holmwood, decapitated, and has garlic stuffed in her mouth.

- **Dr. Jack Seward:** Van Helsing's former pupil, and overseer of his own lunatic asylum which houses bug-eating madman, Renfield, Seward is one of the dedicated party who hunts and eventually dispatches Dracula. It's Seward's keen observations of Renfield and his intense doctoring that makes him one of the most endearing and enduring characters in vampire cinema.

- **Quincey P. Morris:** The sole American in *Dracula*, Morris is a Texan vying for Lucy's hand in marriage. A caricature of the typical American, Morris is replete with American slang, humor, and adages that often break the seriousness of the impending horror. If you want to impress your friends with vampire trivia, ask them which character ultimately kills Dracula. It's Morris who sends Dracula to hell by plunging his Bowie knife into his heart, after which the king of all vampires' "whole body crumbled into dust."

- **Arthur Holmwood:** Of the three suitors pursuing Lucy, the Honorable Arthur Holmwood is the most aristocratic. Partway through *Dracula*, in fact, he becomes Lord Godalming after the passing of his father. With the knowledge that Lucy is to become his wife, Holmwood is, next to Harker, the most motivated to kill Dracula in the name of revenge as, in the end, it's Holmwood who must put a stake through Lucy's heart to give her peace. Like Morris, the character of Holmwood is often ignored in vampire cinema.

- **R.M. Renfield:** In many of the *Dracula*-based films it's Renfield who has completely lost his mind and identity to

Dracula, a fact that makes him one of the more intriguing characters in *Dracula*. Obsessed with consuming spiders, flies, and small birds, Renfield is used as a conduit by Dracula to gain entrance to the asylum. The importance of Renfield is the obvious parallel between his mortal obsession for taking lives and Dracula's immortal obsession for doing the same.

Now that you've learned more about the trailblazers of vampire fiction, what must be investigated is the hotly debated legend of what many claim is the "real" Dracula or what experts more commonly realize as the true-life men whose combined exploits Bram Stoker is thought to have used as inspiration for creating his legendary monster—Prince Vlad Dracul and his notorious son, Vlad the Impaler.

A Tale of Two Vlads

Over the past century, there's been much lively debate over what inspired Stoker in his writing of *Dracula*. If you saw the 1992 film *Bram Stoker's Dracula* starring Gary Oldman, then you probably noticed his warrior persona during the opening scenes. That depiction was of Vlad Dracula, a thirteenth century real-life Romanian prince.

During the mid-1400s, Vlad's father, Vlad Dracul, was the ruler of the Hungarian principality of Wallachia in what is now modern Romania. During his reign, he was invited into the "Order of the Dragon" by the Holy Roman Emperor in Hungary. Vlad Dracul means "Vlad the Dragon," and Vlad Dracula translates to "Vlad, Son of the Dragon."

What most experts generally agree upon is that Stoker named his character for Vlad Dracula. What they don't agree on is if Stoker knew much about the prince's true exploits and his reputation for impaling people on long poles, earning himself the nickname "Vlad the Impaler."

WAS VLAD DRACULA *REALLY* A VAMPIRE?

Through the magic of fictional literature and cinema, Vlad Dracula and his legacy, along with his association with

Transylvania, are inextricably linked in the Western mind to the fictional Dracula and vampirism. Despite Vlad Dracula's alleged cruelties in real life, it must be said that there's no evidence or suggestion in Romanian history or lore that equates Dracula's life or death with vampirism.

What most of us are likely unaware of is that to the people of his homeland in Romania, the legacy of Vlad Dracula is generally considered to be symbolic of national pride and patriotism. Although Dracula was a harsh and unforgiving monarch, he vented most of his wrath on the enemies of his principality of Wallachia, as well as the richest and most dominant nobles in the country.

WHERE THE HECK *IS* TRANSYLVANIA?

So in all the years you've heard mention of Transylvania, did you think it was a fictional country? Indeed, the principality of Transylvania is very real, situated in what is now central Romania, with Wallachia located on its southern borders through which run the Carpathian Mountains.

On its western edge, also bordered by the Carpathians, is modern Moldova (Moldavia), in which the Ottoman Turks often conducted military raids centuries ago. The eastern border was the post of Vlad Dracula's father, Vlad Dracul, where he was charged with protecting the vital economic resources of Transylvania from Ottoman incursions.

The descriptions of Transylvania presented by Stoker in *Dracula* would have meant little without his inclusion of the forbidding Carpathian Mountains on the borders of Transylvania. Running through central and eastern Europe for over 600 miles, the Carpathians are the largest mountain chain in Europe, and—fortunately for the apprehensive tone of Stoker's novel—are also home to the largest populations of bears, lynxes, and of course, wolves, in all of Europe's wild habitats.

THE REAL CASTLE DRACULA

So here's another trivia question for you: Is there really a Castle Dracula, and if so, where is it? The international popularity of *Dracula* and the character's association with Vlad Dracula obviously led to an inevitable public demand to tour the legendary homeland of the world's supreme vampire, and in particular to visit his spooky castle.

Of course, the fictional Dracula's castle near the Borgo Pass is just that—a figment of Stoker's imagination. Located in central Wallachia, the Poenari Castle near the Arges River is considered to be the primary stronghold to have been fortified and used by the real Vlad Dracula in the 1400s.

Originally built in a remote region and virtually inaccessible, Poenari Castle now lies in ruins at the top of a forbidding abutment. The "castle" can be more accurately described as a small fortress, and wasn't large enough to house more than 100 troops for any length of time. The Romanian tourism board has made a thriving cottage industry out of passing off Bran Castle located in the community of Bran as Castle Dracula, primarily because it's readily accessible and offers tours. It has a place in Romanian history as most recently having served as the summer home of Romania's beloved Queen Marie. It's said the castle is currently up for sale, so if you've got a few million bucks to spare, you might consider investing in the fake Castle Dracula!

Live Long and Prosper

Okay. Now that you've learned about the evolution of the vampire, the time has come to analyze and dissect the vampire phenomena in general as well as all the characteristics and superpowers of the quintessential immortal chick magnet. We'll now delve into the basics of what makes Mr. Bad Boy and his kind tick, including their blood obsession, their lairs, how they're created, and that naughty little habit they have of mesmerizing us, among other things, so we bend to their every whim.

Chapter 3

Bite Me!

Imagine for a moment that you're a fang-carrying member of Club Undead. As with all humans, you have the innate need to know how you were born, how you can best survive, and how you make friends and influence people. For the human, that amounts to stories about the birds and the bees, visiting Taco Bell, carrying a large mortgage, and excelling at your chosen career. For the vampire, it means learning you were stalked and bitten by a fiend, turning humans into your own midnight snack, slaying billionaires and acquiring their mansions, and winning friends *and* your lunch using hypnotism.

HOW ARE VAMPIRES CREATED?

No doubt, you're very interested in how bloodsuckers actually become bloodsuckers. The most obvious answer to the question of how a vampire is created is that they become a member of the undead by being bitten by another vampire. Right?

While in the majority of cases that may hold true, a vampire's making is infinitely more complicated than that, with many varieties of transformation put into effect depending on the type of vampire and whether the demon is a beast of legend, literature, or film. Some outer space suckers, for example, vampirize a human's energy by mouth-to-mouth contact rather than doing the neck nip.

Now, you might be asking yourself why it is that certain individuals are predisposed to become vampires. Throughout folklore there are many varied references to the ways in which an individual could become a vampire.

As is common throughout Eastern European lore, candidates for a Romanian vampiric rebirth are those who lead sinful lives or commit suicide. It's also believed that a pregnant woman who permits a vampire to look at her will subsequently give birth to another vampire, but there's little evidence as to exactly how a woman would *know* that she's indeed fallen under a vampire's gaze.

In Romania, the prime revenant contenders are children born out of wedlock, those born with a *caul* (the amniotic membrane of birth that often clings stubbornly to a baby's head), and children who die before baptism. Other legends have it that the seventh son of a seventh son, or the seventh child of the same sex can also be born as vampires.

NO DRAIN, NO GAIN

If you happen to have the misfortune of being the obsession of a typical drawing-room bloodsucker like Dracula or even a modern-day bad boy, then chances are you're intended to become his bride rather than his Blue Plate Special, in which case he would technically become your *maker*, or *parent*.

One crucial thing most vampires have to learn is how much blood to take from a victim. Drawn in small doses, a victim can sustain a vampire for quite some time before either dying or, should the vampire choose, enter the world of the undead. The act of consuming blood is for the vampire a matter of restraint, as the action generally triggers a frenzy that if not carefully controlled usually kills the victim.

Depending on the type of vampire, *bringing* or *crossing over* a victim, or making them a vampire, can trigger various actions. Some vampires gain the memories of their maker, others are left to discover their newfound powers and blood-lust for themselves. In Anne Rice's *Interview With the Vampire*, Louis tells of his making by Lestat's hand, describing being "weak to paralysis," completely panicked, and unable to speak. Once initiated with Lestat's blood, Louis roamed free to see the intensity of the world for the first time with preternatural eyes.

NIGHT OF THE LIVING DEAD

As you now know, the majority of folkloric vampires aren't the pristine, white-skinned, radiant sophisticates created by Anne Rice. As a collective, most are reconstituted corpses in various states of disarray and decay. They're not all like Brad Pitt and Tom Cruise.

Over the centuries, all measure of humanity, from plague victims to nobles to ordinary farmers, have been exhumed and burnt to a crisp in order to expunge their alleged vampirism and keep them from feeding on the living. Which is to say, that given the lack of understanding of decomposition, as evidenced by Peter Plogojowitz and Arnod Paole in Chapter 1, many of these poor souls were unjustly convicted of being in league with the undead.

The Fear Factor

So, knowing what you've already learned about their manipulative ways, do vampires frighten you? As a species that's trained to fear all things that go bump in the night, it would seem obvious that to us humans, a vampire would prove to be our worst nightmare.

Fear is a powerful component of the human psyche, one that feeds off our imagination and lays patiently in wait in the dark corners of our minds like Freddy Krueger at a post-Halloween clearance sale. Vampires thrive on fear and the power they have in controlling it through hypnosis, seduction, or any physical means necessary (see Chapter 4).

Given that the vampiric creatures of lore were often insipid and hideous beasts, it's easy to see why the mere thought of them instantly elicits fear. Vampires in literature approach the aspect of fear with carefully measured words meant to evoke specific imagery and emotional reactions.

Silver screen vampires have arguably given us the most nightmares in that regard. To actually see a vampire in whatever form encircle its prey in a calculated attack or design a slow macabre courtship, then ultimately watch as its fangs pierce through exposed skin leaves a lasting impression both literally and figuratively. Among the many swirling tales of vampirism there are several major factors that play into the terrifying grip these bad boys have on our psyche, including, among other things, plagues and epidemics.

Epidemic Proportions

Throughout history mankind has been burdened by all kinds of incidents deemed epidemic, be it a loss of livestock, crops, accidents, uncontrollable weather, unexplainable deaths, insane behavior, and, of course, various forms of diseases and plague. For all of those occurrences there's typically a need for blame to be placed and retribution taken.

In areas of the world where superstition or strict religious adherence is the law of the land, this approach has been historically prevalent. When plagues strike, the inevitable ensuing hysteria quite often includes accusations of paranormal or supernatural occurrences in order to explain the spreading sickness, or alternately, that the sickness itself causes vampirism.

For example, the very stench of the dying was once considered what we in the modern-era term an airborne illness like a cold or pneumonia. To ward off the stink and alternately repel evil demons, people would surround themselves with pungent odors such as garlic, juniper, incense, perfumes, animal manure, and even human feces.

Vampires, witches, werewolves, and all types of mythological creatures were easily blamed for epidemics, as were outcasts of society, and even children, pregnant women, midwives—practically anyone who by today's standards would in some areas be considered out of society's norms.

Likewise, any stranger who had the misfortune of arriving in a village around the same time people became ill would be highly suspect. During the plagues of the Middle Ages, whether they were bubonic (transmitted by the fleas from rodents), septicemic (blood poisoning), or pneumonic (lung infections and therefore airborne), the undead were among those highly suspect in initiating the illness or becoming undead as a result of it.

Under such circumstances, steps would be taken to identify the culprit (i.e. the earliest infected individual) and stake or burn the corpse, or both, along with various measures taken to spread the ashes in rivers or consecrated grounds (see Chapter 5). What could also contribute to vampiric hysteria is the way in which plague victims were buried: in mass graves, shrouded, without coffins, and some even prematurely. Suffice to say, that whatever the illness, be it widespread or localized, it was easy to blame it on a vampire.

The Blood Is the Life!

If there's one major element that's associated with vampires, it's undoubtedly blood, which begs the question: Who really is responsible for that crucial bad boy practice? Of course, as you've already learned, folkloric critters had all measure of bloodlust, as did the first vampires in literature, but in truth we can blame Bram Stoker for the "veinity" of vampires becoming renowned.

In Chapter Eleven of *Dracula*, Dr. Seward tells of his altercation with Renfield, who after attacking Seward with a knife and cutting Seward's wrist, licked the blood from the floor and began repeating over and over: "The blood is the life! The blood is the life!"

An oft-used phrase in vampiric film and literature, "the blood is the life," is indeed a concept intrinsically linked to the vampire realm on all accounts, from folklore to modern society. Blood is what keeps us functioning. It's the elixir common to all mammalian life forms—one that's cherished, sought after, sworn by, studied, shed, exploited, diseased, spilled, donated, and ultimately revered for its ability to rejuvenate both in a spiritual and physical capacity.

Blood is unique in that it can be offered on many levels: as sacrifice, in absolution, revenge, or in exchange for saving a life or alternately used to take a life. Blood has a rich history that has evolved from our earliest beginnings and continues to flow in all types of creative ways.

For example, did you know that some vampires are not intent on sucking blood? Nope. Some of them prefer instead to drain humans of their psychic or spiritual energy. An individual's life force, their spiritual energy, and their soul are all equally enticing to a sucker, depending of course on the type of creature they are.

HISTORIC SYMBOLISM

As with many other vampire-related aspects such as fire and water, blood is highly symbolic. In all realms, be it spiritual, physical, scientific, religious, supernatural, or meta-phorical, blood has been immortalized and analyzed since the dawn of man.

For starters, there are endless accounts and legends of blood rituals and sacrifices throughout history from the early pagan beliefs of Eastern Europe to ancient Mayan civilization, to centuries of warriors, tribes, practitioners of magic, serial killers, science done in the name of progress, religion, or any number of causes or beliefs.

Warriors, for example, have been known to ingest the blood of their enemies in order to increase their own strength. Like-wise, in the modern era, the Masai warrior tribe of Kenya *ex-sanguinate*, or drain, blood from the jugular of their cows, and consume the blood with milk in the belief that it will give them extra strength.

Perhaps the best known manifestation of metaphorical blood is wine in relation to the blood of Christ. This particu-lar aspect of blood symbolism is arguably the most relevant when it comes to vampires, given the underlying subtext of the vampire as the devil, its practice of usurping blood, which is equated to life, and its typical aversions to holy artifacts like the crucifix, holy water, churches, consecrated ground, and the Eucharist wafer, which is symbolic of Christ's body (see Chapter 5).

The blood representation that Bram Stoker used in *Dracula* is evidence that he likely intended to link its meaning to bibli-cal sources, and many authors over the decades have followed his lead. The phrase "the blood is the life" is from Deuteronomy 12:23 and reads: "Only be sure that you do not eat the blood: for the blood is the life; and you may not eat the life with the flesh." As a black devil and symbolic opponent of God, Dracula in many ways uses blood as revenge against God.

BLOOD AND IMMORTALITY

If you were attacked by a vampiric creature you might en-dure several fates. In many instances, enough blood is sucked by the creature as to cause its victim to perish. Still others lose a substantial amount of blood to cause prolonged illness that eventually ends in death.

At its worst, victims of vampires have enough blood drained from them that they are turned into one of the undead. In literary and cinematic traditions, the ever-present aspect of vampirism as a twisted fountain of youth is often employed by vampires in an effort to assure their victims that immortality is a gift rather than a curse.

Such is the case with Miriam Blaylock, Whitley Strieber's vampire in *The Hunger*, who promises her companions immortality, but can't deliver (see Chapters 6 and 10). In Chapter 4, we go in-depth into the characteristics of the vampire, but there is one trait that arguably stands above the rest in regard to the overall persona of the vampire and his relation to the procuring of blood. Therefore, we introduce here a discussion of hypnosis and the way in which a vampire uses his or her mesmerization skills to best advantage.

The Power of Hypnosis

One of the more insidious and most discussed vampire characteristics is the ability to hypnotize individuals and even create a telepathic bond. It sounds like a cool superpower to have, doesn't it?

Not in this case. More often than not, the transfixed gaze of a vampire results in the victims' full cooperation in giving themselves freely and fully to the fiend's formidable dark gift. In truth, it's a clever tactic and animalistic in its execution. Interestingly, vampire bats impose a similar poise as part of their attack procedure.

With the ability to walk upright, a vampire bat stalks its prey, mesmerizes it, and then heads for the nearest vein in order to pierce it and use its elongated tongue to lap up the blood. As you can see, a bad boy's hypnotic abilities cater perfectly to the inherent dominance and arrogance of his character.

TAKE ME TO YOUR BLEEDER

The greatest benefit of vampiric hypnosis is the most obvious—if you can will another to do your bidding, your ability to ultimately satisfy your arousal or simply procure your dinner becomes infinitely easier. A compliant victim under a vampire's spell typically offers little resistance when the fiend moves to suck the life from him or her. This type of control also makes it easier for a vampire to move about society, travel, maintain living arrangements, and generally obtain whatever it is that he or she requires with minimal effort.

MIND OVER MATTER

The process of mesmerizing an individual first came to prominence with Franz Anton Mesmer during the late 1700s. The term *hypnotism* is associated with the Greek god of sleep, Hypnos.

When Bram Stoker wrote *Dracula*, the "science" of hypnotism would've been known to him and as such he made good use of it in his novel. Many experts, in fact, attribute the vampire's hypnotic ability to Stoker's creation, where it appeared on several occasions, the first of which Jonathan Harker discovered when attempting to strike the sleeping Count with a shovel and was hypnotically driven to flee.

Lucy falls victim to Dracula's remote telepathy as he bids her wake and walk out into the dark night. During the scene in which Dracula baptizes Mina with blood from his chest, Van Helsing declares that: "Jonathan is in a stupor such as we know the Vampire can produce." But it's Mina who's ultimately the one who establishes a mind-link to the dark demon, a fact that's confirmed after Van Helsing hypnotizes Mina and learns through their telepathic link that Dracula is aboard a ship sailing for Transylvania.

Establishing a Lair

Part of being a successful vampire requires a well-honed survival instinct, and where residence is concerned, the same principles that apply to humans apply to vampires: location, location, location! That, and trusted servants, proper lodging that traditionally includes native soil stuffed in a comfy coffin or crate, and a top-of-the-line security system that would make Fort Knox seem like a Circle K.

Of course, that elaborate setup is for the more affluent blood-sucker. For the average sucker, one who's always on the move, in case of emergency a decrepit crypt, mausoleum, cemetery, or abandoned building would surely do.

> In the television series *Forever Knight* detective Nick Knight made ample use of the trunk of his car if the coming dawn found him far from home (see Chapter 11).

It should also be mentioned that vampires who live among each other tend to have more affluent digs. Oddly enough, there doesn't seem to be an expert consensus as to what a group of vampires is called. In film and both fiction and nonfiction they're variously referred to as a *clutch*, a *brood*, or a *coven*. In folklore, they're often referred to as a pack, while in some arenas are also known as a *clan* or divided into *bloodlines*. That said, covens typically have a better security system. The downside to having immortal roommates is that the nocturnal nut jobs can be a permanent pain in the neck!

SERVANTS AND SECURITY

By their very nature, vampires require a certain measure of privacy and security. Being in possession of a creepy remote castle is obviously ideal, or in the case of the modern vampire, a mansion or luxury apartment that affords easy access, maximum security, and foolproof escape routes when the pesky vampire hunters come calling.

In *Dracula*, Stoker portrayed Renfield as a tool, his lunatic persona giving valuable insight to Dracula's London pursuers. Only when the evil fiend arrives in England does Renfield begin to show servitude to the "master."

> In the majority of fictional works and films, a vampire's servants are nothing more than a vehicle for accomplishing the tasks one expects of hired help: arranging travel, monitoring security, and in some cases, helping lure the unwary fly to the web of a famished fiend.

Travel is, of course, of grave concern to the traditional vampire, as many such as Dracula were hindered by the confines of traveling with earth or native soil packed into a crate or coffin (see Chapter 4).

The tricky bit with having servants who are unaware of one's vampiric condition is the necessity of cloaking the basics of normal existence, namely, the lack of conventional food consumption, sleeping during daylight hours, victims being dispatched at one's home and the disposal of said victims, and the inevitable trickles of blood running down one's chin after a meal or leftovers dried on the face during sleep. Of course, much of this can be remedied by putting servants under hypnosis or in some cases, using them as an occasional midnight snack so as to retain their zombie-like state.

Now, that isn't to say that all servants and friends of a vampire are placed under the fiend's spell. Many vampires in both fiction and film have human companions who are well aware of their condition.

In the case of most vampire romance novels, like Stephenie Meyer's tales, you often find human-vampire romantic connections. Meyer's Bella is a young human in love with the immortal Edward (see Chapter 6).

In the aforementioned *Forever Knight*, Nick's coroner friend Natalie was in the know, and despite the fact his second partner Tracey *didn't* know, she was actually in love with one of Nick's undead compatriots and was well aware her paramour was a vampire (see Chapter 11).

From a writing or filmmaking point of view the complications and love stories that arise from having the two species intermingle makes for a more interesting story—one that can either end brilliantly or with a lot of bloodshed.

FAST FOOD

A vampire's need for sustenance is both inevitable and obsessive, and like most creatures in need of food, there must therefore be accessibility, be it the nightclub down the block, or in the case of a traditional bloodsucker, bleeding dry the inhabitants of a nearby village, town, or city where they can feast upon those who are unlikely to be missed.

In folklore, many of the creatures such as the Indian bhu-ta feed on corpses, and therefore spend their time foraging graveyards and cremation sites. Others use the living as a McDonald's drive-through, substituting Big Macs for various internal organs (see Chapter 1).

For the average vampire, meaning those who don't fall into the reluctant vampire category, blood is the life and must therefore be procured no matter the risk of exposure. Modern-day vampires have a much better chance of their dirty deeds going unnoticed if victims are properly chosen and disposed of. It also helps if vampire slayers and various medical personnel and detectives and the like remain blissful-ly unaware that an immortal bad boy or girl is on the prowl.

Smooth Operators

Whether they operate independently or in clans, immortal vampires retain their fearsome reputation largely because of the host of eccentric, evil, and superhuman characteristics they possess.

Just like human bad boys they're utterly irresistible and get you into the same amount of trouble. Although in the vam-pire's case, that trouble could be eternal! Now that you know what an immortal needs to survive, it's time to dig deeper into the traits most prized by the naughty nocturnals, including their manner of dress, physical transformations, powers, and the fangtastic dental work that serves to punctuate their im-mortal mischief.

Chapter 4

VAMPIRE CHARACTERISTICS

As a species, vampires are quite an extraordinary race, with qualities—though basically evil in their construct—that must be admired: efficiency, intelligence, self-preservation, and the fact that most of 'em are wrinkle-free. To understand vampires is to learn of their characteristics: how they appear, where they sleep, why they become one with the bat, wolf, and mist—all the peculiarities that give you a bigger picture of why vampires are the way they are. And bear in mind, that while these powers may be über-cool, they may also become passé after centuries of overuse.

Fangs, Coffins, and Capes, Oh My!

When you think of the physical appearance of a vampire, what do you imagine? A creepy bloke with a pale and pasty complexion? Long skinny digits? Slicked back hair with a widow's peak and a rather intimidating set of canines that make your toes curl?

All that we know—or think we know—about the vampire in regard to his or her typical characteristics and powers is born of the vampiric triad of folklore, fiction, and film. The first two render an historical legacy of vampires and vampirism that, save for the occasional artistic re-creation, is primarily left to your imagination. The third, film, gives you a whiz bang shot in the jugular by actually showing you vampires in all their crimson glory.

Vampires as a species vary depending on what you see or read. A characteristic that may be prevalent in film and literature, for example, may not appear in folklore and vice versa. But one thing is certain—folklore, fiction, and film play off one another and provide inspiration in their presentation of the vampire as a complete picture.

What's commonly asserted when discussing vampiric traits is that many of them are derived from Bram Stoker. For example the notion of sleep and resting on native soil, coffins, and transforming into mist evolve from his conception of Dracula. That said, it's time for you to examine the various characteristics of the average vampire, including dental characteristics, sleeping preferences, various transformative talents, supernatural powers, and fashion sense.

Given that the traditional drawing-room vampire can generally pass for a human save for the pallor of its skin, it's fair to say that if vampires do exist, you'd likely remain blissfully unaware that there was a predator in your midst. Until, of course, it's too late.

FANGS FOR THE MEMORIES!

When one thinks of vampiric figures, it's quite naturally a set of frighteningly sharp pearly whites that first comes to mind. After all, from a purely functional standpoint, *fangs* are the mechanism by which most vampires consume their food. In the traditional sense, a vampire's fangs are sharp, elongated canine teeth, which when bared are a gruesome and an intimately brutal way to achieve sustenance. At their best, fangs most obviously equate vampires to animals; in particular, wolves, bats, rats, and snakes. At their worst, they act as an efficient mechanism for tearing apart their meals.

Early films such as Bela Lugosi's *Dracula* in 1931, and even the 1922 silent film *Nosferatu* didn't show Dracula biting the necks of his victims (see Chapter 7). Hammer Films, on the other hand, had no issue in boldly showing Christopher Lee's dental demons.

Over the decades, both literary and celluloid bloodsuckers have punctured necks with fangs of varying sizes ranging from pin pricks to holes the size of softballs. Stoker described his Dracula as having "peculiarly sharp white teeth," and later in the tale, when Lucy Westenra is first bitten, Mina describes the bite as "two little red points like pin-pricks." Indeed, they were so inconspicuous, that poor Mina believed she caused the wounds with a big safety pin when securing a shawl around Lucy's neck!

In James Malcolm Rymer's *Varney the Vampyre*, Sir Francis Varney is described as having "fearful looking teeth—projecting like those of some wild animal, hideously, glaringly white, and fang-like."

In many modern-day vamp flicks, the dark devils retain all measure of killer chompers, with some that completely mutate and dominate their faces when bared. In *Blade II*, bloodsuckers infected with a vampire virus become "Reapers," who feed indiscriminately on both the living and the undead. With the lead vamp taking the rat-like features of Count Orlock's *Nosferatu* one step further, Reapers are quite possibly some of the most frightening and voracious vampires ever imagined. They don't just have fangs, they have multiple eel-like tongues that slither out when their chin splits apart, opening up their face to accommodate spikes within their cheeks that latch onto their victims necks and faces. Yikes!

MANICURE ANYONE?

The first sign of a vampire in desperate need of a manicurist is Count Orlock in *Nosferatu*, whose demonic digits are intentionally and abnormally long and gruesome, which adds dramatically to his rodent-like appearance (see Chapter 7). Other than various B-movie bloodsuckers sporting exceptionally long and hideous fingernails while in their transformed states, most traditional Draculas are shown to have some measure of length to their nails, which are usually well manicured.

In Chapter Two of Stoker's *Dracula*, Jonathan Harker includes in his initial description of the Count that his hands had first seemed rather "white and fine" but that upon closer inspection, "I could not but notice that they were rather coarse, broad, with squat fingers. Strange to say, there were hairs in the centre of the palm. The nails were long and fine, and cut to a sharp point." By contrast, Anne Rice's preternaturals have fingernails that are translucent as glass.

Bring Out Your Dead!

When it comes to burial practices there's enough information to fill an entire book, as customs and technology have evolved since cavemen roamed the planet. Early methods of burial didn't make use of coffins as we know them today. Instead, the dead were left to the elements, placed in caves, buried under rocks, set afire, or simply wrapped in a shroud and interred in shallow graves. Naturally, this left corpses vulnerable to the attack of the vampires of folklore like the Hindu *bhuta*, a mythological spirit that lurks in burial grounds and takes possession of them.

The concept of having a coffin, funerary box, or crate, is generally believed to have been a logical necessity in keeping animals—or in the case of folklore, all measure of vampiric creatures—from disturbing the dead. No doubt the existence of cemeteries, mausoleums, and crematoria partially evolved from this thinking as well as the basis for profit in the funerary industry.

COFFINS

Traditional coffins likely evolved during the 1600s in the form of boxes and later as increasingly more elaborate caskets for anyone who could afford them. As such, coffins were a common burial chamber in the late 1900s and the concept was of use to Bram Stoker in creating a resting place for Dracula. During Jonathan Harker's imprisonment at Castle Dracula, he happened upon fifty boxes piled atop newly dug earth, and it was in one of those boxes he discovered the sleeping Count—who didn't necessarily require a coffin per se, but did need to rest amid native soil.

The aspect of all future vampires needing a coffin likely arose from Stoker's initial premise. Even some practitioners of modern-day real-life vampirism prefer to sleep in coffins. True vampire aficionados will likely never forget the eerie yet slightly comical emergence of *Nosferatu*'s Count Orlock from his rat-infested soil-filled coffin aboard the ship *Demeter*. In one swift movement, the stiffened vampire arose from his coffin—a maniacal unblinking mannequin from the bowels of hell itself.

Since that classic silent film, the cinematic and literary vampire have both been characterized as snoozing in coffins and typically shown emerging from them with sinister fingers slowly opening the lid!

As a result of requiring such specific sleeping quarters, the vampire is also restricted to lugging a coffin around wherever it goes. This is evident in early vampire fiction and film. Given that it's not the easiest bed to transport, the use of a coffin is one that many modern authors and filmmakers have modified, or even dropped in their vampire sagas.

Anne Rice's bloodsuckers, for example, don't need coffins (though when they use them it's more for show than substance), instead simply requiring a dark sanctuary such as a crypt, a basement, or even a place in which they can bury themselves for up to centuries at a time when hibernating, as Lestat does from 1929 to 1984 before awakening to become a brash rock star in *The Vampire Lestat*. Likewise, Whitley Strieber's vampires in his 1981 novel *The Hunger* have no aversion to daylight, and therefore slumber comfortably in beds.

NATIVE SOIL AND SLEEP

When it comes to sleep, seemingly invincible bad boys, in general, are relegated to slumber just like the rest of us mere mortals, which in truth, is one of a vampire's few consistent vulnerabilities. The only difference is the vampire's rest is more trance-like and affords various levels of awareness depending on whether it's a creature of folklore, fiction, or film. That awareness is often instilled so as to give the dozing fiend a method of defense in case of an unwelcome intruder. In *Dracula*, Stoker writes of Dracula's sleep during Jonathan Harker's incarceration at Castle Dracula:

> *"There, in one of the great boxes, of which there were fifty in all, on a pile of newly dug earth, lay the Count! He was either dead or asleep. I could not say which, for his eyes were open and stony, but without the glassiness of death, and the cheeks had the warmth of life through all their pallor. The lips were as red as ever. But there was no sign of movement, no pulse, no breath, no beating of the heart."*

Given that the creatures of folklore and Bram Stoker set into motion the idea that vampires must rest between dusk and cock's crow, meaning the onset of dawn, it's fair to say that it's a practice that's endured in traditional vampire legends. The primary reason would suggest that vampires need rest in order to rejuvenate themselves and perhaps as a peaceful respite to fully digest their liquid lunch.

Following Harker's initial discovery of the Count, he documents an attempt at hitting Dracula with a shovel while at rest, but as the shovel is about to strike, Dracula exerts his influence over Harker to avoid the full impact. This reinforces the concept of awareness during vampiric sleep and a kind of hypnosis that caused Harker to flee the scene. The above excerpt also suggests the alleged importance of resting in native soil.

Throughout vampire lore there also exists the concept of *consecrated ground*, a term primarily associated with various religious sanctities whereby an individual is buried within lands considered holy; for example, a churchyard. The practice is most common in Catholicism and significant in the sense that certain deaths, such as suicides, are deemed unacceptable for holy interment.

For vampires, the practice of sleeping on native soil can pertain to the soil of their homeland or in some cases the earth in which they were originally buried. Of course, if they were originally interred in consecrated ground, that creates an issue, given that by rights a vampire wouldn't be able to tolerate holy soil. Thus is the conundrum created by Bram Stoker in asserting that Dracula didn't need to actually sleep in a coffin, but did require a bed of native soil.

In her historical horror series, author Chelsea Quinn Yarbro—who many credit with revolutionizing vampire romance—concocted a unique way for her vampiric protagonist Count St. Germain and his minions to stay in touch with their roots. Rather than sleep in native soil, they place it in a hidden compartment within the heels of their shoes (see Chapter 6).

While many early literary vampires made use of the practice, others did not. Neither James Malcolm Rymer's fiend, Sir Francis Varney, nor John Polidori's Lord Ruthven or even Anne Rice's Lestat and company require a coffin or native soil. What Stoker created with the trapping was a plot confinement whereby Van Helsing could gather his troops and search for Dracula knowing that he could be found in one of fifty earth-filled boxes that could then be filled with Eucharist wafers to pollute the soil.

For some of the folkloric vampiric creatures native soil was a necessity, though the majority who were shape shifters could easily enter and exit their grave via a hole dug in the ground. For the most part, modern-day vampires are rarely hindered by the confines of their native soil. If you happen across an otherworldly hunk whose cologne smells of freshly turned soil, however, be afraid. Be very afraid.

SUPERHUMAN POWERS

As a physical presence, vampires by all accounts are, without question, entirely intimidating. And they should be given the varying range of "superpowers," if you will, that they can possess. Most vampires as evolved from Dracula have some of these abilities, including superhuman strength; physical agility; acute vision; a magnified sense of smell, vision, and hearing and the abllity to hypnotize others and to shape shift rapidly.

Add to that what's been introduced in literature and a range of films, including vampires who can fly, levitate, become invisible, time travel, employ telekinesis, use telepathy, heal, move with extreme speed, cast spells, withstand sunlight, or even cause spontaneous combustion. If you had all of these powers, wouldn't you be tempted to join your undead boy toy and live for all eternity?

STRENGTH

One of the characteristics common to most all vampires is superhuman strength coupled with extreme physical agility. After all, they need those abilities in order to overpower their prey, fight attackers, and elude capture. In the Hammer films, for example, it's quite common to see Christopher Lee tossing an attacker across the room with the strength of a dozen men.

More modern-day vampires, like Blade, Violet in *Ultraviolet*, and Selene and her kind in *Underworld* not only possess otherworldly strength, but the ability to perform *Matrix*-like jumps and acrobatics across great heights and distances. Still other vampires are able to spend some time in daylight, though their powers may be greatly reduced.

Stoker's Dracula also had the ability to scale walls like Spiderman, a tradition carried on by Gary Oldman's homage in the 1992 film, *Bram Stoker's Dracula*. Romance novelist Linda Lael Miller's bloodsuckers have the freedom to time travel at will, while some of Anne's Rice's ancient vampires have, in addition to strength, the gift of flight, and in the case of Akasha, Maharet, and Marius to name a few, the destructive ability of setting afire and obliterating inanimate objects or immortals.

As the vampire genre continues to evolve in the literary and cinematic realm, so too do the powers that vampires possess. Because of the growing list of vampiric powers, there must also be new means of destroying them. For example, in the *Underworld* films, vampires can be vanquished with the clever use of ultraviolet ammunition in liquid form, with the lycans likewise succumbing to bullets filled with liquid silver nitrate (see Chapter 8).

The one thing that remains consistent in regard to a typical vampire's strength, and ultimately all of their superpowers is blood or in some cases, energy. As their lifeforce, a vampire must maintain their blood or energy consumption or risk losing everything. "The blood is the life," and without it, a vampire will weaken to the point of starvation (see Chapter 3).

PLAY MISTY FOR ME

In the 1931 film *Dracula*, Mina Harker describes to her husband "John" Harker a terrible dream she had, and that when the dream came: "It seemed the whole room was filled with mist. It was so thick, I could just see the lamp by the bed, a tiny spark in the fog. And then I saw two red eyes staring at me and a white livid face came down out of the mist."

In the same film, Renfield describes a similar encounter: "A red mist spread over the lawn, coming on like a flame of fire. And then he parted it, and I could see that there were thousands of rats with their eyes blazing red like his only smaller."

The two scenes brilliantly illustrate the apparent concept that Dracula possesses the ability to become mist—a power that preys upon our debilitating fear of that which we cannot lay eyes upon. Who knows what lurks within the fog? And worse yet, how easy is it for mist to creep under doorways and seep through small cracks and crevices? Of course, if you're immortal boyfriend needs to sneak into your bedroom, that could come in handy.

The use of mist as a harbinger of evil in the vampire realm is quite common and has been effectively used in both literature and an abundance of films. In Stoker's *Dracula*, the doomed ship *Demeter,* carrying the vampire on board, becomes awash with mist, and Van Helsing himself asserts that: "He can come in mist which he create, that noble ship's captain proved him of this, but, from what we know, the distance he can make this mist is limited, and it can only be round himself."

In *Dracula*, it's Mina Murray who's most plagued by the mist, whereby in Chapter Nineteen, while safely stowed in her quarters, she writes that during what she perceives to be a dream she notices a white mist creeping toward the house with "almost perceptible slowness," a whirling mist that enters her room forming a cloudy pillar with lights that "seemed to shine on me through the fog like two red eyes." For Mina, that would be the last time the fiend appeared to her by means of mist.

There's no doubt that Stoker made great use of mist as one of Dracula's powers. It is, and most likely shall remain, a permanent fixture in the horror genre, but Stoker wasn't the originator of the vampire as mist.

Creatures of lore and legend were often tracked and identified by means of grave markers and any unusual characteristics of their final resting place. In some cases, the sign of a vampire would be suspected if small holes were noticed around their burial site, indicating that an evil creature had the means to possibly become mist and move freely in and out of the grave without disturbing it.

ALTERING WEATHER

Many superstitions and rituals throughout history have been based on controlling or predicting weather. Think Groundhog Day, Native American rain dances, and the fact that your crummy knee joint can predict an upcoming frost. In the vampire realm, controlling weather has little to do with superstition and everything to do with it being a super-cool power to have.

In truth, Stoker's study of superstitions is likely what caused him to make mention of Dracula's ability to alter weather patterns, an ability that's shown up in a number of vampire films, quite blatantly in Coppola's *Bram Stoker's Dracula* in 1992. On the upside, if your nocturnal boyfriend is planning a midnight picnic, full control of the weather will prove beneficial.

What's in a Name?

As you learned in Chapter 2, it's a logical assumption that Bram Stoker came across the word *Dracul* as part of his research on Transylvania and learning of Prince Vlad Dracul and his son Vlad the Impaler, aka Vlad Dracula.

Dracul, meaning "son of the dragon," would seem an appropriate name for a predatory preternatural mythical creature who can fly. One also has to wonder how coincidental it was (it wasn't) that Van Helsing bears the name of the author —*Abraham*—its shortened version being *Bram*.

In an attempt at trickery, the name *Alucard* has also been used on numerous occasions, *Alucard*, of course, being *Dracula* spelled backwards. This was used by Lon Chaney Jr. in the 1943 film *Son of Dracula* as well as other films including *Dracula A.D. 1972*, and the animated Hellsing trilogy. Author Sheridan Le Fanu employed a similar tactic for his vampiric ingénue Carmilla, who is also known as Countess Mircalla Karnstein.

Dressing the Part

As you can see, vampires in folklore, fiction, and film have many commonalities and just as many obscurities and eccentricities. As discussed, the mere mention of the word *vampire* conjures up the traditional Dracula ensemble of a black tux and/or tails, a long opera cloak, and the occasional hint of red. While this image is almost entirely attributed to Irish playwright Hamilton Deane and his 1924 adaptation of Stoker's novel (see Chapter 7), it's also been set in stone by a number of films, not the least of which is Lugosi's appearance in *Dracula*.

Whether he's known as a Count or Prince, the mere designation of Dracula as royalty—as with many other fictional and celluloid vampires—lends itself to his wearing attire befitting an aristocrat. After all, who would suspect an impeccably dressed gentleman to be a deviant, bloodthirsty vampire?

FIENDISH FASHION

In literature, especially in historical horror and vampire romance, that trend continues, with vampires ranging from Count St. Germain to Lestat costuming themselves with the styles of their era, as any intelligent undead predator would do in order to blend in with the general public. Some vampires, however, refuse to go with the flow.

Anne Rice's Marius, for example, wears rich velvet jackets no matter the era. Where vampires tend to get more specialized with their attire is in film, especially in the action crossovers. In the *Underworld* films, Kate Beckinsale's Selene is a cool drink of water in her black skintight leather unitard and long coat with accentuated cape-like flow. In *Ultraviolet*, Milla Jovovich does her comic-book alter ego justice with her instantly interchangeable slick attire and hair colors reminiscent of Sydney Bristow in *Alias*.

Even Van Helsing has rolled with the fashion punches. In the 2004 blockbuster *Van Helsing*, dashing Hugh Jackman is fabulously clad in an ensemble harkening back to the heroes of the Wild West with a black hat, and a long black leather coat and duster. Who knew Van Helsing could look so hip?

WHAT'S WITH THE CAPE?

One of the most instantly recognizable traits of the vampire, aside from the gleaming, blood-dripping fangs, is its cape. Typically long, heavy, and black with the occasional red lining, the cape is highly symbolic in its representation of the bat. As mentioned, the adding of a cape to the Dracula persona is the brainchild of playwright Hamilton Deane, who no doubt felt that Dracula's cloaked gentleman fiend would make for great impact in theatrical performances. He was spot-on.

The cape has become an iconic part of the Dracula legend, its long swishy fabric allowing him (or her!) to move with ease and giving rise to one of the vampire's most famed positions—that of pulling the cape up to his face and over his head so as to completely hide himself and blend into the shadows.

A Howling Good Time

As you've probably ascertained, the vampires and vampiric creatures of folklore are a decidedly mixed bag of humans, zombies, animals, and various hybrids and mutants. In many ways, the creatures of lore are more primal in their conception and definitely more animalistic in their hunting and killing of victims than vampires turned from humans. Bear this in mind when debating whether or not to have a vampire boyfriend or go to the Humane Society to adopt a Chihuahua.

While vampires are often associated with a number of different animals, among them cats, dogs, birds, and various insects, they're most commonly linked to bats and wolves. And while many animals can become vampires, they can also be enlisted to help combat vampires. Horses, for example, are used in graveyards to locate a vampire's resting place.

GOING BATTY

It's no small mystery that the vampire bat is associated with the legendary bloodsucker. Primarily found in Central and South America and a few areas of the southern U.S., the vampire bat is small in size but bears a particularly frightening appearance that complements its disturbing feeding habits, including an erect stance, large eyes, teeth that are incredibly sharp, and a lower lip possessing a cleft.

As mentioned earlier, it is indeed a blood drinker with tactics similar to that of a vampire in that it feeds at ground level, and attempts to hypnotize its prey before glomming itself onto a vein and lapping up blood with its long tongue. With saliva containing an anticoagulant, the bat is able to keep blood flowing until it's sated. Like vampires, they must maintain blood intake or face rapid deterioration.

The bat has appeared in legend and lore for centuries, but didn't become famous until Bram Stoker brought it to the forefront. Stoker made free use of the bat in *Dracula*, as it appeared at the windows of Renfield, Lucy, and the Harkers. Subsequently appearing in Lugosi's *Dracula* (in what many still dub the "yo-yo bat" for its jerky movements), it quickly became one of the most definitive icons of the vampire.

And just in case that isn't creepy enough, meet *Calyptra thalictri*, otherwise known as the vampire moth. No lie. It's said that a bite from the moth gives it the ability to fill its stomach with human blood, leaving swelling and pain in its wake. No doubt a bug zapper might help you drive off the latest and greatest in vampiric predators.

HUNGRY LIKE THE WOLF

In Chapter Two of *Dracula*, when Jonathan Harker sits with the Count after his arrival at Castle Dracula, there is, in the background, the sound of wolves howling. It's at that point the black demon utters arguably the most famous line of the novel: "Listen to them, the children of the night. What music they make!" By all accounts, it's a chilling statement, one that over the decades has been repeated many times with varying alterations. Dracula's almost gleeful acknowledgment of the wolves is a devilish way of paying homage to folkloric beasts while also hinting at his ability to become a wolf himself.

EMBRACING YOUR INNER BUFFY

Throughout vampiric folklore a wide range of mechanisms, rituals, superstitions, weaponry, and religious implements have been employed in an effort to rid the living of the undead. Some of those deterrents remain in common use by vampire writers, filmmakers, and the occasional modern-day vampire hunter, while other new and advanced techniques have evolved with various films and fictional works.

It's time for you to take a deep breath, clear your mind, and again call forth your inner Buffy because we're now introducing you to the methods you can use to protect yourself from the onslaught of a bloodsucker and, more importantly, what you can do to destroy it.

Chapter 5

COMBATING AN
IMMORTAL BAD BOY

Let's say for a moment that you're being stalked by a vampire. How do you protect yourself? What weapons do you need in your supernatural arsenal? Most importantly, how can you destroy the sucker? Fortunately, there are many different methods and implements that are purported to work, ranging from a vampire's abhorrence of garlic and its fear of certain religious items, to decapitation and driving a stake through the creature's heart and burning the corpse. Prepare yourself for a Buffyesque battle. Grab your torch, your holy water, and your sharpest Manolo stilettos, and pray you keep your jugular intact.

How Do You Fight a Fiend?

When it comes to the legendary triad of witches, werewolves, and vampires, there's never an easy way to rid yourself of their malevolence. Witches can call upon black magic, spells, and all kinds of sorcery. Werewolves have all the creature comforts afforded a wild animal and can strike and stalk with zero inhibition.

Vampires have a bit of both, but their circumstances are hindered by a multitude of deterrents and relatively well established ways to kick the bucket. In the case of many fictional and cinematic vampires, they often succumb to death, and wait until they can be resurrected through magic, blood ritual, or all sorts of imagined reanimation recipes.

Bear in mind that while it *is* possible to destroy a vampire, keeping them at a distance—if only temporarily—is a much safer option. Over the course of centuries, through folklore, fiction, and film, we've become well acquainted with a host of items that can be used to deter creatures of the night.

Some of these objects—for example garlic or crucifixes—may not necessarily kill an immortal, but they are thought to offer some protection against them. After all, no vampire hunter worth his or her salt would fail to have crosses, garlic, holy water, stakes, a few memorized Bible passages, and a way to create fire readily at hand.

Now in qualifying the items and methods you're about to be introduced to, it must be said that much of this applies to the traditional vampire.

As society has evolved, so has the vampire and its aversions, superpowers, and the ways you can destroy it. What may repel or kill the bloodsucker of legend may prove ineffective on a wide range of modern fiends—from the soul suckers and plague vamps to the exotic and predisposed blood drinkers on P.E.T.A.'s hit list.

The bottom line with any vampire who *doesn't* fit the traditional mold is the good old trial-and-error method of discovering what they're repelled by and what their weaknesses are.

For starters, that would still include the basics, and the tried-and-true methods of yesteryear. With that in mind, let's begin by taking a look at what might help in your quest to protect yourself from a dastardly demon of the night.

Practical Protection

Speaking from a highly logical and practical standpoint, there are several items that you might simply have around the house that can, in many cases, repel the traditional vampire or act as a testing ground for a modern-era vamp. Garlic, salt, candles, incense, and even bells, among other items have in the past been proven effective against vampires.

GOT GARLIC?

It's likely you have garlic in your kitchen. We're not talking the crusty, dried-up, powdered crap at the back of your spice cupboard. We're talking nice fat, fresh bulbs of the stinking rose. Garlic is one of the most commonly thought of items used to ward off the majority of vampires, and a protection device against evil that's existed since ancient times.

A member of the lily family, garlic contains natural healing powers and has long been used for medicinal purposes as well as herbal uses, but as a vampire deterrent it's arguably second to none as a first line of defense. Additionally, it can be used in the destruction process.

Throughout folklore and in Stoker's *Dracula*, a vampire's mouth is stuffed with garlic after beheading, and a corpse's mouth is similarly filled to prevent its joining the undead. In *Dracula*, Van Helsing fills Lucy's entire room with garlic flowers and bulbs, even rubbing it all over the door jamb and fireplace to keep Dracula from entering.

Vampiric folklore is rife with individuals making use of garlic as a repellent. Given that a vampire's senses are heightened, particularly its vision, hearing, and smell, it stands to reason that garlic—whether it's worn around the neck as a wreath;

strewn around a house; rubbed onto a human, animal, or object; or even liquefied and sprayed—would be enough to keep the undead at bay.

SALT AND SEEDS

As a matter of superstition, there are still many of us who subscribe to several practices. Do you knock on wood? Avoid stepping on a crack? Toss salt over your shoulder for luck or to ward off evil? In the case of the latter, there's good reason to keep it on hand in case of vampiric incursion.

Salt is a staple of ancient and modern history especially in regard to the supernatural, paranormal, religious, and, of course, the culinary realms. Throughout history, salt has been used as a means of preservation both with food and in the form of natron, which the ancient Egyptians used for perfecting the mummification process.

Salt also serves as a symbol of purity and a means by which you can repel evil. In some legends, the undead cannot cross a line of salt, in which case windows, doors, fireplaces, and entire houses were often surrounded with an unbroken line of salt if vampires were thought to be on the prowl.

Like salt, seeds are often used as a vampire repellant. While mustard seed is the most prominent—possibly for its religious connection as mentioned in one of Jesus' parables— other small seeds and grains like poppy, oats, millet, and carrot to name a few, can also be used, as can the thorns gathered from wild roses.

One theory is that if a vampire encounters the seeds, they're required to count each seed before coming to a village to procure victims. Some folkloric tales mention that the vampire can count only one seed per year, so even a small handful of the seeds would keep evil at bay for long periods of time. Another speculation is that they can become so caught up in obsessively counting the seeds that they lose track of time and are forced to retreat as the sun begins to rise!

Seeds as well as salt were also sprinkled in and around corpses and coffins to prevent vampirism or keep a vampire from rising from the grave.

Hallowed Weapons

In many vampire legends, religious icons play a prominent role in defending against the undead. Considering the representation of evil that Bram Stoker made his fiend, it makes sense that "good," as represented by such items as a crucifix or holy water, holds sway over him. Stoker used this underlying theme prominently in *Dracula*, but not all writers have continued this tradition, and the effectiveness of religious weapons against a vampire varies.

In the film *Interview with the Vampire*, Louis de Pointe du Lac flat out tells his interviewer that he's rather fond of crucifixes, a common theme among modern vampires who often mock and scorn frightened mortals who attempt to fend off attack using a holy artifact. To some, the power of a crucifix or holy water exists only if *you* believe—and the undead would be unlikely to believe. Nonetheless, hallowed weaponry such as crosses remain, much like garlic, an integral part of vampire lore.

CROSSES AND CRUCIFIXES

One of the most often used weapons against a vampire is a cross or crucifix, which is a cross bearing the figure of Christ hanging from it, and represents Jesus' crucifixion on Good Friday. The crucifix is primarily a Roman Catholic symbol, with other Christian religions preferring a plain cross, representative of Christ after the crucifixion.

It's said that a crucifix has more power than a cross, but again, in both cases its energy is largely dependent on how strongly the person holding it believes in its symbolism. In *Dracula*, Stoker brings the crucifix into the mix beginning in

Chapter One, as a confounded Jonathan Harker has a rosary with a crucifix forced upon him by a villager as he awaits his departure for Castle Dracula. Harker, of course, being an "English Churchman" believes the crucifix to be somewhat idolatrous.

In the 1960 film *The Brides of Dracula*, Van Helsing (played by Peter Cushing) makes innovative use of a windmill against David Peel's evil Baron Meinster. Van Helsing jumps on the windblade, carefully turning it so as to create the giant shadow of a cross which on the ground below confines and effectively helps destroy the Baron (see Chapter 8).

In traditional lore, the crucifix will burn the skin of the vampire when pressed against it, and mark the flesh of a person who has been bitten but not yet fully transformed into a vampire. Additionally in some legends, the crucifix or cross will steal the creature's source of strength, rendering it less powerful. Some stories claim that crosses or crucifixes hung on a door will keep a vampire from entering a room or that a cross placed on a gravesite will make it impossible for it to enter the grave.

Perhaps the best thing about crosses is that they're easily improvised using items such as candlesticks, swords, random bits of wood—anything that can replicate its crossed positioning. In more contemporary vampire tales, however, crosses and crucifixes, while typically used in some measure, often present no threat to a vampire's existence.

HOLY WATER

As one of the primary symbols of life, water retains its power as a spiritual and physical cleansing mechanism and one of the strongest proponents of life itself. We spend our first nine months immersed in water and indeed our bodies are almost entirely comprised of water.

However, the undead have little use or respect for water—especially that which has been blessed. Used in many religious ceremonies such as baptisms and absolution rites, holy water, which is blessed and made sacred by the clergy—especially in the Catholic and Eastern Orthodox churches—is believed to have special powers and uses. Among them is the ability to repel most unholy creatures—including vampires.

Because holy water is pure and blessed it's said to burn the flesh of the demons like acid burns human flesh, causing extreme pain and peeling burns. In the case of newly created bloodsuckers, this could prove fatal. Throughout vampire lore, when bodies of suspected vampires were exhumed, holy water was often used in the rituals meant to keep the undead from rising.

In the same vein, it was also sprinkled atop a grave or over a coffin to prevent its inevitable return. Much like salt, holy water can also be sprinkled or poured onto window sills and doorways to prevent a vampire from entering. In film and fiction, holy water is typically tossed onto a bloodsucker from a vial or flask. In a pinch, even a perfume atomizer might prove helpful!

EUCHARIST WAFERS

The Eucharist wafer is yet another religious symbol that is thought to offer protection against vampires, though it's not as commonly mentioned as crosses or holy water. The wafer, which is a thin piece of blessed bread, represents the body of Christ in the Holy Communion ceremony.

Like a crucifix, the wafer can burn the flesh of a vampire, and leave a mark if pressed against the skin of its victims. In Chapter Sixteen of *Dracula*, Van Helsing, after finding Lucy's empty coffin, shocks his cohorts by finely crumbling up wafers, combining them with putty, and using the mix as a sealant around the door to Lucy's tomb. When asked what the mixture is, he replies that it's "the Host," which he brought from Amsterdam.

In Chapter Twenty-Two, he again makes use of the wafer on several occasions, the first in an effort to keep Mina from further harm. When he touches the wafer to her forehead, however, she screams as her skin becomes seared as if touched by "a piece of white hot metal." After that incident, the hunting party proceeds to Carfax and are faced with Dracula's boxes of earth. Van Helsing then proceeds to open the soil-filled boxes, lay the wafers upon the earth, and reseal them to prevent Dracula returning to them.

Mirror, Mirror, on the Wall

One of the more shocking aspects—or at least it was until it became a hallmark of the drawing-room vampire—is the concept that bloodsuckers cast no reflection in a mirror. If the eyes are indeed the window to one's soul in a metaphorical sense, then the inability to see one's own reflection speaks to a lack of soul. This begs the question of whether or not vampires even have souls, other than one doomed to eternal damnation or to ultimate absolution once their curse is lifted.

In the 1992 film *Bram Stoker's Dracula*, the latter concept seems to apply upon Dracula's death, an appearance of final absolution, if you will, as we don't actually see him carted off kicking and screaming to the bowels of hell. His face at the time of death is flooded in white light, suggesting a heavenly ending. On the other hand, in Stoker's novel, the destiny of eternal damnation is more likely, as one can argue that Dracula is more deeply entrenched as an evil figure rather than a romantic one, and his death results in his crumbling to ashes.

The mirror aversion likely spawns from Stoker's *Dracula*, and after it was published, it quickly became an accepted part of the vampire legend. In Chapter Two, Jonathan Harker makes note in his journal that Castle Dracula is devoid of mirrors. Later in that chapter comes one of the more chilling scenes of the book: Harker is shaving using a small shaving mirror when the Count comes up behind him. He casts no reflection, a fact that does not go unnoticed by Harker, who has cut himself, nor to the dark devil who reacts to the blood running down Harker's chin, the rosary he wears, and the mirror.

How Do You Destroy a Vampire?

Vampires, as with all revenants, exist in a strange dichotomy. They're no longer living, and they're no longer dead—they're undead. So, if you're stuck in a *Night of the Living Dead* situation and you lack the cool weaponry that a cinematic Van Helsing possesses, what do you do?

For starters, you have to know what kind of vampire you're dealing with. Is it a traditional stake-through-the-heart preternatural fiend, an outer-space soul sucker, or a genetically mutated biological-warfare-gone-wrong plague pusher? If it's the latter two, you may have to do a bit of experimentation to ascertain a method of destruction, but what's curious about all types of fictional and cinematic vampires is that almost always there exists a way of killing them by traditional means, even if those ways may be somewhat disguised.

WHAT'S AT STAKE?

Perhaps the most common method associated with destroying a vampire is staking it through the heart. No doubt, it's a procedure that's been well-used throughout literature and film, as it makes for a spectacular end to an unearthly villainous rampage.

Though the practice of staking was introduced in early literature, particularly Sheridan Le Fanu's "Carmilla" (see Chapter 2) and Stoker's *Dracula*, the concept of using a sharpened stake is entrenched in not only vampiric folklore, but the legends of numerous other revenants as well.

The idea of driving a stake through a corpse was born of the typical folkloric propensities devised for dealing with the undead and the efforts undertaken to make certain they didn't rise from the grave. In some traditions a buried body would have a stake driven completely through it to hold it into the ground, with some cultures going so far as to drive spikes or thorns through the tongue to prevent the alleged vampire from using it to draw blood.

Other legends describe stakes pounded in the ground above a grave to ensure that a reanimated corpse was staked if it attempted to arise from the earth, its head staked to secure it to the ground, and even staked through the back and buried face down to prevent it digging its way up and out. Traditionally, stakes are handmade, finely sharpened, and usually made of local hardwoods felled from trees such as juniper, whitethorn, hawthorn, ash, wild rose, or buckthorn.

Curiously, some legends make mention that a stake is only to be hammered into the chest in one blow, for if it's struck twice, the revenant can reanimate and return to its vampiric state.

One of the benefits of staking, aside from the obvious relief that you can at last get a night's rest without worrying about someone latching onto your neck, is that in many instances it's reported that after the staking, the screaming, and the inevitable blood spurting, the corpse's face often relaxes to show relief.

But staking a vampire doesn't necessarily mean he or she can't be resurrected. In the 1970 film *Taste the Blood of Dracula*, Christopher Lee's Dracula is burned to cinders. Later that year, in *Scars of Dracula*, the same ashes are bled upon by a leaky, blood-engorged bat and lo and behold, it's enough to resurrect the king of all immortals! The same principle applies to Blacula in the 1973 sequel *Scream Blacula Scream*, whereby a voodoo spell results in Blacula's bones acting as a conduit to his groovy resurrection (see Chapter 8).

LET THERE BE LIGHT

Another common form of vampiric destruction is, of course, sunlight. Given that vampires are reanimated undead corpses who in most cases have no beating heart and are cold as ice, the warmth of the sun stands in direct contrast and therefore provides an easy mechanism for you to play "burn baby burn." But that convention doesn't always apply.

A host of folkloric suckers are able to move about during daylight hours as well as both traditional and modern-day vamps in both fiction and film. The Bulgarian vampir, for example, is a reanimated corpse that moves to a new village. It lives normally by day, but becomes a monster by night.

In *Dracula*, Bram Stoker twice allows Dracula to appear during daylight hours, though his powers are greatly diminished. Whitley Strieber doesn't even go that far with his immortals in *The Hunger*. They have no issue whatsoever functioning in daylight, as does Blade, in part due to his hybrid human-vampire disposition.

Arguably the most evil twist to the destructive capabilities of sunlight is the fact that it's quite often used by vampires to kill other vampires. In *Interview with the Vampire*, Anne Rice makes use of this, assigning the fate to Claudia and her keeper Gabrielle for Claudia's attempts to kill Lestat.

In the film *Underworld*, vampire elder Viktor bestows the same fate on his daughter Sonja for carrying a child conceived with the lycan leader, Lucian. Since that time, many cinematic and literary vampires have alternately suffered from a daylight aversion or been given the power to embrace it, or in the case of Anne Rice's vampires, Armand, in particular, the choice of flying into the sun to commit suicide. Curiously, moonlight has played a factor in bringing vampires to life. In John Polidori's *The Vampyre*, Lord Ruthven is reanimated after giving order that his corpse "be exposed to the first cold ray of the moon that rose after his death." Le Fanu's Carmilla is also rejuvenated by the moon's rays.

ALL FIRED UP

As far as fire is concerned, it's one of the mainstays of human survival since the dawn of humankind. It keeps us warm and works in food preparation. It's also used as a method of destruction as the by-product of both accidents and Mother Nature. Even further, fire is often used by witches, sorcerers, shamans, holy men, and all measure of conjurers for both good and evil.

In the metaphorical realm, fire, like water, is a characteristic means of cleansing or purification. Biblically speaking, fire is entrenched in symbolism, not the least of which is God appearing to Moses in the form of a burning bush. With all of that history behind it, fire has both a good and bad reputation in what it provides. In vampiric folklore it's often used as one of the means for combating evil, though how it's used is largely dependent on its effectiveness.

Folkloric creatures were often exhumed and their bodies burned to ashes. For the most part, this is the safest way to assume a vampire is indeed dead. But in the modern era, that's most definitely *not* a sure bet.

More than a few fictional and cinematic vampires have been resurrected despite having been reduced to a pile of ash or with even a small portion of their ashes serving as the catalyst. The same goes for threatening a vampire with fire. Given that many vampires have regenerative capacities that allow them to quickly recover from things such as stabbings and gunshot wounds, setting one on fire doesn't provide a guarantee of destruction.

In the 2004 film *Van Helsing*, for example, Dracula is violently thrown into a huge burning fireplace by Frankenstein, only to walk out of the flames with his burnt face quickly returning to normal. As a rule, cremating a revenant is always worth a try, but be warned that in this case, the ashes-to-ashes and dust-to-dust rule should be heeded with extreme caution. Err on the side of reason and release the ashes into the nearest river.

WATERWAYS

As previously discussed, water is one of the primary symbols of life, and while holy water can do damage to a vampire, unblessed water has a different set of benefits, many of which apply to other revenants such as witches as well.

One commonly held folkloric belief is that vampires cannot cross over running water, nor can they swim across it. As seen in Stoker's *Dracula* and many other incarnations, they can be carried over water by means of a ship. That vampires can actually drown is debatable, as some legends suggest that though a vampire cannot swim, it would suffer no ill effects if pulled from the water.

One film in particular, the 1966 *Dracula: Prince of Darkness*, made good use of this legend by having Christopher Lee's bloodsucker become submerged in icy waters, only to be resurrected in *Dracula Has Risen From the Grave* (see Chapter 7). Still other folkloric legends have it that vampires and other revenants can be banished to remote islands surrounded by water, thereby assuring they have no means of interacting with society and could even die of malnourishment. Salt water in these instances provides a twofold measure of protection as vampires are also repelled by salt.

OFF WITH YOUR HEAD!

As folklore and common logic would dictate, it would seem that decapitation would be the most obvious and permanent means of destroying a vampire. For that reason alone, all good Buffys keep a machete close at hand! For the most part, beheading a dark devil does indeed do the trick, but there are a few caveats.

In the case of modern vamps, the same rules sometimes apply as with fire. If a vampire possesses the power of regeneration, then it's conceivable that they're able to reposition their head upon their neck and allow everything to reattach itself. Throughout folklore, corpses were very often beheaded with the head being burned along with the body or removed and even buried separately with the mouth stuffed with garlic. Many suspected vampiric corpses were also treated to a garlic stuffing.

However, the concept that those exhuming and burying the corpse had to pay heed to is the fact that if you decapitated a vampire, the head should be placed nowhere near its neck or especially its arms, which could conceivably move the head back where it belongs.

The Vampire Hunter's Kit

One of the most intriguing and continuing mysteries of the twentieth century involves the manufacture and sale of vampire-killing kits attributed to a Professor Ernst Blomberg of Germany, with antique percussion-style pistols made by gunsmith Nicholas Plomdeur of Liege, Belgium, supposedly dating from the late 1800s.

A number of Blomberg's kits have turned up in recent years, and some have sold for rather astonishing amounts, including one at Sotheby's that went for $12,000 in 2003. The Sotheby's kit consisted of a walnut box with a hinged lid, housing an antique pistol, ten silver bullets, a wooden stake and mallet, a crucifix, a rosary, and several vials of garlic powder and various demon-thwarting serums. The authenticity of Professor Blomberg's kits has come under a fair amount of scrutiny in recent years, with very few reliable results, and even less hard evidence that he even existed.

There is, however, anecdotal evidence that vampire-killing kits became fairly popular in England and western Europe soon after the release of Bram Stoker's *Dracula* in 1897, that were supposedly made for nervous travelers to Eastern Europe, but more likely concocted as souvenirs. Nevertheless, most of those kits were quite well made and expensive, and designed for the well-to-do who had a penchant for unusual contemporary novelties.

Although early vampire hunters in Eastern Europe made do with shovels, hand-carved wooden stakes and a mallet, and an axe for decapitating the unsuspecting undead, the self-respecting vampire hunter of today wouldn't be caught dead without an arsenal of demon dispatching tools close at hand. Nor should you. That said, if you're planning on embarking on a career as a slayer, there are a few mandatory items you'll need to assemble:

- **A Wooden Box:** Preferably made of ash or hawthorn wood with a cross carved into the lid so as to dissuade inquisitive vampires from snooping inside.
- **Stakes:** For the record, just about any stake or sharp, pointed object should suffice, but according to lore, any local hardwood such as ash, hawthorn, juniper, wild rose, whitethorn, or buckthorn is ideal. In some cases, silver

stakes can also prove useful depending on the type of vampire you're facing.

- **Crosses or Crucifixes:** In keeping with your wooden box and stakes, crosses or crucifixes should be made out of ash or hawthorn wood to add to the aversion level.
- **Holy Water:** Most vampire hunters carry holy water around in vials or flasks. A spray bottle adjusted to squirt a steady, vamp-searing stream might also prove helpful.
- **Fire:** Traditional vampire hunters typically rely on matches, candles, and torches. A few butane lighters, and maybe a small blowtorch would seem a bit more reliable— and dramatic.
- **Mirrors:** A tried and true repellent—at least according to vampire cinema. Irritated vampires are notorious for smashing mirrors, so you'll definitely want something shatterproof and larger than your compact unless you're using it to reflect sunlight in a precisely directed burn.
- **Garlic:** Probably the most common standby, vampires hate garlic with a passion. Fresh garlic powder, garlic cloves, garlic anything. There's no such thing as too much garlic.
- **The Bible:** Another vampire-hunter favorite. Threatening a vampire with the Holy Book while reeling off a few choice verses is a standard vampire-hunter tactic.
- **Poppy or Mustard Seeds:** Because vampires traditionally have an obsession with counting grains, tossing a handful of seeds in its face should keep a vampire occupied for hours, which should give you enough time to fire up the torch.

Now, be warned that the aforementioned items are the basic kit elements of the well-prepared Buffy wannabe, and nothing less will do in the face of a vampire intent on slurping you dry. And, don't forget to wear a fashionable scarf to protect your jugular, which will probably be pulsing at a delectably galloping rate. So now that you've got the tools, how do you go about trapping a vampire?

How to Catch a Vampire

In Wes Craven's 2000 film, *Dracula 2000*, Van Helsing (Christopher Plummer) came up with an innovative way to ensnare Dracula (Gerard Butler) by making use of the basics. Leading the demonic sucker into a dark London alleyway, Van Helsing disappeared into a doorway. Dracula, attempting to follow him paused, sensing something was afoot.

At that point, Van Helsing reappeared in Dracula's view as he reached out in front of him to discover that what he was staring at was a mirror. Given that Dracula casts no reflection, Van Helsing was actually standing *behind* Dracula and immediately brought down iron bars around the fiend to form a prison cell. Pretty slick, eh?

NAILING A NEFARIOUS NIGHT STALKER

For the most part, one of the best methods of catching a vampire is to corner them in such a way that you can expose them to sunlight, torch them, or even drown them, as was done to Christopher Lee's Dracula in *Dracula: Prince of Darkness*. The key is making use of whatever weaponry or on-the-fly ingenuity you can conjure up at that very moment.

In Frank Langella's 1979 *Dracula*, for example, Dracula's last stand in the hold of a ship gave Van Helsing the opportunity to entangle and hoist the sucker upward to the top of the mast to burn in the sun's rays.

In *Dracula 2000*, a similar method was employed, with Mary Van Helsing wrapping cable around Dracula's neck and falling with him off the edge of a building. She watched from below, as Dracula (aka Judas Iscariot) dangled from the building and burnt with the rising sun (see Chapter 8).

BAIT AND SWITCH

For many literary and cinematic vampires, especially in classic films, the standard form of destruction is finding the vampire at rest and staking it through the heart. That tidy set-up doesn't necessarily work on all modern-day vampires. The most important concept every vampire hunter needs to grasp, just like any hunter, soldier, or chess master, is how to assess and capitalize on your opponent's weaknesses.

For the sci-fi vampire it may require a genetically self-mutating form of intergalactic Ebola. For the comedic ber-serker it could mean dressing like Bozo the Clown and shoot-ing a holy water pistol. For the folkloric incarnation you might have to reanimate its natural predator. Whatever the situation, it's safe to say that there are no steadfast rules in destroying a vampire. The best you can do is start with the basics and go from there to find what works.

The Highgate Vampire

Although the modern vampire hunter is a relative oddity in comparison to the ubiquitous slayers of old Eastern Europe, one of the most infamously well-known vampire hunts oc-curred at Highgate Cemetery in London in 1970, and it was conducted not by a single intrepid hunter, but two competing "vampire slayers" who've repeatedly faced off to deal with the Highgate phenomenon.

David Farrant and Sean Manchester investigated the ru-mors that a vampire was on the loose and soon began feuding over who had the best plan to capture it. Although no proof was *ever* found that the vampire even existed, Farrant and Man-chester attracted enough media attention to create a minor uproar that started a mob scene of "vampire hunters," roam-ing through Highgate Cemetery. Farrant and Manchester have each capitalized on their reputations as genuine vampire hunt-ers, and continue their feud to this very day.

Watch Your Ash!

As you've now learned, immortal bad boys and girls are in-finitely more complex creatures than you might expect, each one possessing its own powers and capabilities that are largely drawn from folkloric revenants, early vampire literature, and cinema. Of course the only way you can protect yourself from a vampire, uncover its weaknesses, and potentially destroy it, is to learn how to detect and slay it.

That said, it's now time to shift gears and delve into the vampire of modern literature. By reading some of these terrific novels and series, you'll gain further insight into how you can deal with any situation involving a vampire. Oh, and along the way fall in love with a host of addictingly romantic rogues.

Chapter 6

The Literary Vampire

Just as with film, the literary community has over the decades embraced the vampire in all its preternatural glory. From its earliest inception to the present day, vampire literature has had myriad resurrections, with bloodsuckers taking all types of forms spread across all genres, from serialized novels based on television series, to comedies, to Westerns, to gothic and modern romance and historical horror. Delve into any of these wonderful novels and you'll quickly be transported to another place and time along with some of the most romantic and notorious characters in literature.

Out of the Shadows

In Chapter 2, you learned about early vampire literature and the trailblazers—Bram Stoker, John Polidori, James Malcolm Rymer, and Sheridan Le Fanu—who set the standard for all literary and cinematic vampirism to come.

Now it's time to take a peek into the modern-day literary realm and all the movers and shakers who have shaped, and continue to maintain, the evolution of the world's most enduring immortal bad boys and girls. The sheer volume of vampire literature stands in tribute to the fact that no matter what era, what genre, or what type of vampire is imagined, audiences never lose their taste for bloodsuckers.

Les Vampires de Anne Rice

Of the hundreds of thousands of dedicated writers who've put pen to page over the centuries there are but a few who have risen to the level of Anne Rice, who over thirty years ago brought to life the most influential vampire since Stoker's *Dracula*.

During the course of her career Rice has unleashed upon the world a family of vampires known simply by their singular names: Louis, Pandora, Armand, Marius, Maharet, Merrick, Akasha, and Magnus, to name a few. But it wasn't until the beginning of her literary endeavors in 1976, and the masterpiece *Interview with the Vampire* that we were first introduced to the intensely emotional preternatural ebb and flow that *is* the vampire Lestat.

Not since *Dracula* have the collective hearts, minds, and souls of the public been drawn to a vampire whose seductive charm, wicked intellect, philosophical nature, and excruciating thirst to reconcile good and evil make him a true vampire of the ages. Unlike Dracula, Rice instilled in Lestat de Lioncourt—her ultimate hero—a deep and unbridled emotion matched only by the wisdom he so desperately seeks whether it be in his understanding of his reluctant fledgling Louis de Pointe du Lac, the teachings of Marius and Talamascan David Talbot, the destructive capacities of the ancient Akasha, or his confrontations with God and the alleged devil himself in *Memnoch the Devil*.

It's said that Lestat was based on both Rice and her husband, Stan, with the very idea of *Interview with the Vampire* coming to Rice as a result of her five-year-old daughter, Michelle, succumbing to a rare form of leukemia. In life, Lestat was from an aristocratic lineage fallen on hard times during the 1780s. Born as a vampire by Magnus in the latter part of the 1700s, Lestat is, in all his vanity and bold endeavors, the quintessential vampire of the modern era.

Complex and luxuriously rich in their conception, their lineage, and their powers, Rice's *la famille de vampires* are most certainly the most revered in history. Rice has told their tales in what are the renowned *Vampire Chronicles*, including: *Interview with the Vampire, The Vampire Lestat, The Queen of the Damned, The Tale of the Body Thief, Memnoch the Devil, The Vampire Armand, Merrick, Blood and Gold, Blackwood Farm, Blood Canticle*, and additional tales including *Pandora* and *Vittorio the Vampire*.

Add to that, their crossover into her bestselling series of the Mayfair Witches. Like Stoker, Anne Rice set the standard for all vampire fiction to come, and in her life's work she can, above all, take pride in knowing that she and her beloved vampires are *all* truly immortal.

Popular Vampire Fiction

During the mid-1970s, the most popular vampire novels foreshadowed the concept of the vampire epic, with Anne Rice's *Interview with the Vampire* becoming the first of the *Vampire Chronicles*.

Beginning in 1978, we were given only a hint of the towering efforts and prodigious talents of Chelsea Quinn Yarbro when she introduced us to what would become the St. Germain series. Tales of Yarbro's impossibly "human" vampire have been in nonstop evolution for thirty years and there's no sign of St. Germain disappearing into that cold dark night.

WELCOME TO THE *HOTEL TRANSYLVANIA!*

Yarbro's first effort in the series, *Hotel Transylvania*, is set in the French court of King Louis XIV in the mid-seventeenth century, and features the Count of St. Germain, who's been a vampire for hundreds of years, and manages, unlike most vampires, to maintain a sense of superior humanity over bloodlust.

In sharp counterpoint to Rice's vampires, or to those of virtually any other author, Yarbro's St. Germain is suave, sophisticated, and genuinely concerned about other human beings; in effect, he's a vampire with a soul. He's acutely aware of the frailty of human life, and does his best to respect the living, while abhorring the evils that mankind brings upon itself.

To paraphrase Yarbro's personal perspective on the subject of the eternal vampire living in a world of mortals, her unusual approach to the vampire condition is to consider how a rational being would realistically react to the dilemma of being threatened with permanent alienation from mankind.

Yarbro's sympathetic approach to the vampiric experience cast a new light on what was previously assumed to be an inherently evil transformation. Unlike Dracula, and in fact unlike most vampires in lore and literature, St. Germain "treasures the brevity of human life rather than holding it in contempt."

For millions of transfixed readers, the lack of gore and violence in Yarbro's work has hardly been a dull literary experience. In fact, it's instead proven to be life-affirming and poetic. Yarbro's twentieth book in the saga, *A Dangerous Climate*, was published in September 2008.

The influences of Anne Rice and Yarbro spawned a renewed interest in all things dripping crimson. Here are some of the notable authors who followed in their footsteps:

- *The Vampire Tapestry* by Suzy McKee Charnas (1980)
- *Fevre Dream* by George R.R. Martin (1982)
- *Vampire Junction* by S.P. Somtow (1984)
- *Those Who Hunt the Night* by Barbara Hambly (1988)
- *The Golden* by Lucius Shepard (1992)
- *Children of the Night* by Dan Simmons (1992)

A WHOLE *LOT* OF SALEM

The prodigious and prolific talents of horror fiction icon Stephen King were put to use in 1975 with his second published novel, *Salem's Lot.* King is said to have begun the novel after pondering what would happen if Dracula re-emerged in twentieth-century America.

The result was a truly creepy story set in the sleepy town of Salem's Lot in rural Maine, and involved a series of disturbing occurrences and missing children that coincides with the arrival of newcomer Kurt Barlow, who now inhabits an old house with a lurid past. Soon the entire community is overrun as townspeople are transformed into vampires one by one.

The protagonists in the book are eventually forced to leave Salem's Lot to the vampiric infestation, although they do manage to destroy Barlow before taking flight. *Salem's Lot* has the unusual distinction of having been made into *two* television series; one in 1979, and the second in 2004.

Although King originally called the town "Jerusalem's Lot," the publishers shortened the title to "Salem's Lot" because they felt the original title carried a religious connotation.

FEEDING *THE HUNGER*

Taking a fascinating and fresh approach to the vampire novel, Whitley Strieber created one of the most enduring images of the cold, calculating vampire in *The Hunger*, published in 1981.

The last of her species of a bloodsucking alien race, vampire Miriam Blaylock has lived for thousands of years, and is in the habit of taking human lovers and turning them into companions—but cannot make them truly immortal (see Chapters 6 and 8). Although Miriam has the power to turn humans into vampires, she lacks the capacity to give them everlasting life such as hers, and manages to increase their lifespan by only a few centuries; a tragically short time frame from the perspective of a timeless being.

After *The Hunger*, Strieber stepped away from the vampire genre and concentrated on speculative fiction and books concerning his own alleged contact with aliens. Twenty years after its publication, however, Strieber returned to the saga of Miriam Blaylock, with *The Last Vampire* in 2001, and again in 2002 with *Lilith's Dream: A Tale of the Vampire's Life*.

The Hunger was made into a cult classic film in 1983, starring Catherine Deneuve, David Bowie, and Susan Sarandon. Although there are several variations between the novel and the film, one of the most significant differences is that in Strieber's original story, Miriam Blaylock lives on to continue her hideous legacy (see Chapter 8).

THE HISTORIAN

It's interesting to note that one of the bestselling books of 2005 was a vampire novel. In *The Historian*, first-time novelist Elizabeth Kostova brought *Bram Stoker's Dracula* into the modern era by excerpting significant chunks of Stoker's novel and working it into her own historical plotline.

In *The Historian*, a teenage girl living in Amsterdam discovers in her father's library an ancient book which is blank save for a woodcut of a sinister dragon on one page with the word *Drakulya*. The discovery leads to a long search for Dracula, and once again Vlad Tepes comes into the picture—this time with truly spine-chilling results. He's not simply as the inspiration for the vampire Dracula, but the still living personification of the father of all bloodsuckers.

BLEEDING HEARTS: THE ROMANTIC VAMPIRE

Perhaps no other character in literary history is better suited —and more destined—to become the subject of pure romantic fiction than the inherently sexy and alluringly charming vampire.

It's no surprise that in the field of romance, vampires have taken a huge bite out of the estimated $1 billion in annual sales generated by the romance genre and the 41 million enthralled readers who blissfully bleed for their favorite heroes and heroines whether they be alive or undead. What follows is a list of some of the most popular series of romantic vampire novels to capture the imaginations and hearts of a devoted readership:

- The *Riley Jenson* series, by Keri Arthur
- The *Cassandra Palmer* series, by Karen Chance
- The *Nightwalker* series, by Jacqueline Frank
- The *Night Huntress* series, by Jeaniene Frost
- The *Gardella Vampire Chronicles*, by Colleen Gleason
- The *Guardians of Eternity* series, by Alexandra Ivy
- *Forever and the Night, For All Eternity,* and *Time Without End,* by Linda Lael Miller
- The *Little Goddess* series, by Amy Lane
- The *Brotherhood of Blood* series, by Kathryn Smith
- The *Companion* series, by Susan Squires
- The *Darklyn* series, by Lynn Viehl

PARANORMAL NOSFERATU

Vampire fiction took an inevitable turn into the literary subgenre of paranormal romance in 1986 with the publication of

Jayne Ann Krentz's *Sweet Starfire*. The blending of romance, science fiction, and traditional horror created an unforgettable mixture of blood and lust in a far-away galaxy of pure fantasy, and authors who embraced the concept have never looked back.

These vampiric novels have crossed virtually every line of fantasy and science fiction to tap into an endless supply of mysterious locales and fantastic supernatural abilities that quite literally know no boundaries.

ANITA BLAKE: VAMPIRE HUNTER

Beginning in 1993 with *Guilty Pleasures*, Laurel K. Hamilton's *Anita Blake: Vampire Hunter* series has developed a legion of die-hard fans since its inception. In Anita's parallel universe, she reanimates the dead for a *living*, by working for Animators Inc. as a necromancer, raising and healing long-dead zombies, vampires, and werewolves in a series of sixteen hair-raising novels, the latest of which is the 2008 offering *Blood Noir*. During the first five books, Blake remained remarkably celibate, but by book number ten, she was beginning to let it all hang out, and romantically intimate interludes have become a minor, although graphic, element of her adventures.

DARK AND DEADLY

Since the beginning of this century, novels in the paranormal, romantic, and vampiric veins have exploded both in popularity and in the sheer volume of titles printed. Christine Feehan has virtually owned the paranormal vampire romance genre, beginning in 1999 when the incredibly successful *Dark* series captured the imaginations and hearts of millions of spellbound readers. In her first book, *Dark Prince*, Feehan's construction of an ancient race of emotionless shape shifting vampires, the Carpathians, who can find salvation only through discovering a life mate and true love, set the stage for a string of twenty novels, several of which have been huge bestsellers and have garnered Feehan a clutch of literary awards.

SOUTHERN BITES

One of the most well respected authors of paranormal vampire fiction, Charlaine Harris developed her writing chops on two stand-alone novels before considering attacking books in the increasingly popular series approach to character development. Harris's initial foray was with the *Aurora Teagarden* series beginning in 1990 that dealt with the sleuthing of a Georgia librarian into mysterious murders. Harris's second series was the creation of the *Shakespeare* mystery novels in 1996 that again dealt with basic mortal mysteries.

Harris hit vampiric paydirt with the introduction of Sookie Stackhouse in the *Southern Vampire* series beginning in 2001 with *Dead Until Dark*. The first installment won the prestigious Anthony Award for best paperback mystery the year it was released, and paved the way for seven more bestsellers to follow.

Harris's Sookie Stackhouse is a young telepathic barmaid in northern Louisiana genetically imbued with "faerie" blood, which may explain her telepathic powers and her unfortunate ability to attract the unwanted attentions of unearthly beings, including vampires and werewolves. Much of the series is dedicated to Sookie solving supernatural mysteries, as well as handling the dilemmas of personal relationships with members of the netherworld who've integrated into society with the invention of manufactured synthetic blood.

Harris's latest book, *From Dead to Worse*, published in May 2008 remains a bestseller, and the entire series has developed a loyal following of die-hard fans who are no doubt soaking up *True Blood*, the new HBO series based on Harris's novels (see Chapter 11). Here then are the books in Charlaine Harris's popular *Southern Vampire* series:

- *Dead Until Dark* (2001)
- *Living Dead in Dallas* (2002)
- *Club Dead* (2003)

- *Dead to the World* (2004)
- *Dead as a Doornail* (2005)
- *Definitely Dead* (2006)
- *All Together Dead* (2007)
- *From Dead to Worse* (2008)

Comedic Bloodsuckers

It may be difficult to imagine that a mix of vampiric blood-sucking and humor could go hand-in-hand, but just as the preternatural creatures of the night have crept into science fiction, romance, and historical fiction, they've also made pretty tasty fodder for some bloody fun reading.

Death by the Drop, by Timothy Massie, is a fairly recent 2008 addition to the relatively small list of vampire novels with distinctly humorous undercurrents that literally drip with sarcastic wit.

The reigning matriarch of wickedly vampiric fun is unquestionably Mary Janice Davidson, whose *Undead* series of hilarious books feature the irrepressible Betsy Taylor as a former model and recently unemployed single woman who finds herself flattened by an SUV and comes back to life a vampiress. Rather than taking to the life of the walking dead, "Queen Betsy" attempts to resume her less than normal existence of stocking up on designer shoes and trying to find a job. Of course, Betsy is also sidelined by irritating conflicts with evil vampiric beings who have absolutely no sense of humor. Books in Mary Jane Davidson's *Undead* series include:

- *Undead and Unwed* (2004)
- *Undead and Unemployed* (2004)
- *Undead and Unappreciated* (2005)
- *Undead and Unreturnable* (2005)
- *Undead and Unpopular* (2006)
- *Undead and Uneasy* (2007)
- *Undead and Unworthy* (2008)

YOUNG ADULTS AND THE LIVING DEAD

Literature for young adults has been a booming element of the publishing world since the early 1800s, and one of the most predominant themes has always been fantasy and horror. Although children's fairy tales are generally considered to be fairly mild fare for kids, many of the concepts, such as in the story of Little Red Riding Hood, were pretty harrowing in their day, (especially given that the first versions of the tale simply ended after the wolf had devoured Red Riding Hood and her granny). Even Bram Stoker took a turn in 1881 at writing fairy tales in the compilation, *Under the Sunset*, which was often considered far too disturbing for impressionable minds.

Most modern young adult literature features teens as the major characters, and fictional forays into the world of the undead are no exception. The book series that followed television's *Buffy the Vampire Slayer* is one case in point, with the ultimate Valley Girl, Buffy Summers, continuing her crusade of monster mayhem against the forces of evil.

But, in the netherworld of young vampire literature, no one holds a candle—or a crucifix—to Stephenie Meyer and her thoroughly absorbing *Twilight* series of heart-pounding sagas.

MOVE OVER, HARRY POTTER

Although Anne Rice has developed a literary reputation as the original "Queen of the Damned," Stephenie Meyer has achieved her measure of notoriety and success in the young adult market as more of the "Queen of the Darned." In a marked departure from the sexual undertones of much youth-oriented literature, Meyer has sidestepped the hormonal rages of growing up to provide a series of wildly popular books featuring teenaged heroine Bella Swan and her continuing relatively coy relationship with the irresistibly considerate and impossibly gorgeous boy vampire, Edward Cullen.

In the original self-titled book of the *Twilight* series, published in 2005 and written when Meyer was twenty-nine years old, Bella Swan moves from sun-soaked Phoenix, Arizona, to the damp and dreary town of Forks, Washington, to live with her father. On her first day in school, Bella notices the ethereally handsome and secretly vampirish Edward Cullen staring at her with a blood-chilling glare while the phrase "if looks could kill" suddenly runs through her mind.

As it turns out, Cullen isn't offering a threat—he's just primordially fascinated by her smell. Through the next three novels to follow, the pair fall deeply in love and survive painful separations and harrowing scrapes with evil vampires and other creatures of the night.

INNOCENT BLOOD

The innocent nature of Meyer's novels is no accident. As a devout Mormon and mother, she insists that much of the sex, drinking, and violence of young adult literature upsets her, and she directs her work to the vast audience of youngsters—particularly girls—who don't identify with or haven't experienced the darker side of adolescence.

For Meyer, her characterization of Bella is that of a nice, normal girl, whose boyfriend is attentively and irreproachably respectful. Meyer's unique approach struck a positive chord with an enormous fan base, and the *Twilight* series is giving the popularity of Harry Potter a run for supernatural supremacy. Books in Stephenie Meyer's *Twilight* series include *Twilight* (2005), *New Moon* (2006), *Eclipse* (2007), and *Breaking Dawn* (2008).

THE ENORMITY OF THE BUFFYVERSE

In all of vampiredom in the twentieth century, there may be no single phenomenon with a broader sweep than the kick-butt adventures of Buffy the vampire slayer (see Chapter 11). Resulting from the 1992 film of the same name the enormously popular *Buffy* series ran for seven seasons. *Buffy* became one of the most successful vampiric dramas in televised horror. It triggered the television spinoff *Angel*, and dozens of spinoff original and graphic novels. The list of installments is seemingly endless, and the sheer number of tales told in various *Buffy* compilations dwarfs those of any other vampiric figure in fiction.

The list of authors who've contributed to *Buffy* fiction is a virtual "who's who" of spin-off fantasy writers, including Rebecca Moesta, Mel Odom, Yvonne Navarro, Nancy Holder, and Scott Ciencin, most of whom have contributed to novelizations of well-known cinema classics and media tie-ins such as *Jurassic Park*, *Charmed*, *Star Wars*, *Battlestar Galactica*, and *Godzilla*, along with their own original works.

One prolific *Buffy* contributor, Christopher Golden, has developed a strong following with his *Shadow Saga* series of vampire novels that follow the trials of modern-day vampire Peter Octavian and his kin, known as the "Defiant Ones," who are forced into bloody conflict with humanity.

THE HEARTBEAT GOES ON

The intensity of interest in the supernatural in the young adult market has become a publishing phenomenon, and it shows no signs of letting up any time soon. Perhaps part of the charm of many of these supernatural chronicles is that they describe everyday situations, and put vampire characters into them. As new and expanding plotlines begin delving into other areas of preternatural beings, there have been popular spinoffs into fascinating characterizations of zombies, werewolves, faeries, and ghosts.

Through it all, there's little doubt that vampires are on the leading edge of the paranormal, perhaps because they're not just inherently sexy, they're *dead* sexy.

There are a number of enduring vampire series in the young adult market that you might enjoy, and each of them has their own throng of avid supporters and fans. Here are a few of the most popular:

- The *Chronicles of Vladimir* series, by Heather Brewer
- The *Vampire Kisses* series, by Ellen Schreiber
- The *Morganville Vampires* series, by Rachel Caine
- The *Vampire Academy* series, by Richelle Mead
- The *House of Night* series, by PC Cast
- The *Bluebloods series*, by Melissa De La Cruz
- The *Vampire Diaries* series, by Lisa Jane Smith
- The *Night World* series, by Lisa Jane Smith
- The *Cirque du Freak* series, by Darren Shan

Preternatural Explosion!

Okay gals, with all the valuable vampiric info you've learned so far, it's time to open the crypt to the incredibly vast arena of the cinematic vampire. In regard to film, the vampire is as old as the medium itself, having begun in the Silent Era, continuing to flap, fang, and seduce its way into our hearts and veins to the present day. We begin with the genesis of celluloid suckers, who in no small measure gave us our first solid impression of the vampire and what he or she is capable of. The resulting works have forever changed the vampire genre.

Chapter 7

THE GENESIS OF CELLULOID VAMPIRES

If you're a fan of vampire novels, then no doubt you're a chick who loves vampire flicks. In this chapter, you'll learn the very genesis of vampiric cinema, a success due to several factors, namely the making of the 1922 silent film *Nosferatu*, the 1920s stage adaptations of *Dracula*, and the legacy begun by Hammer Films and their incredible stature in classic horror cinema. So polish up your fangs and prepare to be hypnotized by one of the most popular characters in movie history, and the story of how the vampire first flew onto the silver screen.

Bloodsucking Cinema

It's no mystery that the filmmaking industry since its inception over a hundred years ago has opened our collective hearts and minds to a seemingly endless array of stories that serve to broaden our horizons, transport us to worlds unknown, and ultimately keep us perpetually entertained.

Each movie genre, and every conceivable genre crossover serves to appeal to audiences of all ages who usually find what they're looking for in a film, from a good laugh or cry to a taut thriller, historical epic, or documentary.

There is one genre, however, that stands apart from all others in that its presentation throughout the decades has hinged on one single commonality—fear.

Horror films have a rich history featuring a wide range of tales that prey upon the innate human curiosity surrounding all things that shock, creep, scream, howl, bite, vanish, fly, mutate, and generally move to scare the knickers off us.

Filmmakers who first brought *Dracula* to the big screen set in stone the idea that as a cultural medium, the vampire's tale, as with many other genre-specific characters, has the ability to reflect—in both blatant and subliminal methods—what's occurring in society during various eras. It also retains the mesmerizing hold *Dracula* keeps on its devoted audiences.

During the fifties, sixties, and through the mid-seventies, it was England's Hammer films that capitalized on vampirism in all its red-blooded glory. More importantly, and perhaps not as well known, is the fact that the 1920s stage plays for *Dracula*, written by Hamilton Deane and a later revamp by John L. Balderston, have the distinction of having solidified the trademark characteristics that the majority of cinematic vampires continue to display to the present day. That said, it's time for you to take a peek at one of history's most famous bad boys. But be warned—this nightcrawler is more Freddy Krueger than Brad Pitt.

SILENT BUT DEADLY

There's little argument that no other novel in history has achieved such acclaim as Bram Stoker's 1897 masterpiece, *Dracula*, which has sold millions of copies throughout the past century and launched a franchise of entertainment on both the literary and theatrical fronts.

It is within the film industry that *Dracula* has achieved its greatest popularity, serving as the impetus for more commercially successful films than any other literary work in history. Tragically, that success is an inescapable irony, given the fact that Stoker died in relative poverty never realizing the true cinematic immortality of his legendary creation, whose inspiration began in the Silent Era not long after his death in 1912 (see Chapter 2).

Ironically, the first depiction of Dracula in film is linked not only to Stoker, but his wife, Florence, and her fight to have the film destroyed. In the Silent Era, it is a film that stands alone in its popularity among vampire aficionados and if you haven't seen it, it's well worth a look.

NOSFERATU: THE SCOURGE OF BREMEN

One of the most well-known and revered vampire movies in history is also one of the few silent films to survive the inevitable ravages of time. Made in Germany and released in 1922, it is *Nosferatu, eine Symphone des Grauens,* the literal translation of which means *Nosferatu: A Symphony of Terror.* But it's better known by a single word: *Nosferatu.* Directed by renowned German director Friedrich Wilhelm (F.W.) Murnau, with a screenplay penned by Henrik Galeen, *Nosferatu* is an expressionist film, meaning its director was given to overuse of special effects, which proved to be engaging and utterly frightening in its time, and remains so to this day.

Nosferatu is an unauthorized version of Stoker's *Dracula*, with its characters and geography altered so that the major settings are changed from Transylvania to Bremen, Germany. As is immediately obvious to anyone viewing the film, it wasn't altered enough.

Names of the characters were freely (and not very adeptly) altered; for example, Jonathan Harker became William Hutter, Mina Murray was Ellen Hutter, Renfield was known as "Knock," and Dracula became Count Graf Orlock (also spelled Orlok). The ploy was used in an effort to avoid copyright infringement, a fact that did nothing to stop the inevitable legal battle that would come at the hands of Stoker's widow, Florence. With the aid of the British Incorporated Society of Authors, Florence Stoker served the film's producers with an injunction resulting in the 1925 ruling that the negatives and all copies of the film be destroyed.

Obviously, a few copies survived as the first American release came around 1929. (In both earlier and later releases of the film, the character names are changed to Stoker's original characters.) After that, the film went into relative obscurity until the early 1970s, and has since gone on to achieve cult status.

FRIGHT AND FLIGHT

What makes *Nosferatu* so memorable, aside from its silent screen quirks and on-location settings, is by far the character of Count Orlock, played by German actor Max Schreck. (For an added dose of irony, the word *schreck* is the German word for "fright.") Unlike the suave, debonair, tail-coated Draculas we would be treated to in the decades to come, Orlock is more in keeping with the heinous vampires of folklore. The term *nosferatu* is derived from the Greek word *nosophoros*, which translates to "plague carrier."

Truly ugly in his conception—due in no small part to the film's art director Albin Grau—the unblinking Count has an almost rat-like appearance, with long claw-like fingers, a bald head, hollowed face, pointed ears, exceptionally long rodent-type fangs, and a legion of devoted rats.

By all accounts, Orlock is positively grotesque and void of any of the social graces we associate with the classic drawing-room vampire. When Orlock's English real estate representative Thomas Hutter accidentally cuts his thumb with a knife, for example, Orlock moves to actually lick the blood from Hutter's wound. It's a moment that truly sets up the animalistic reality of Orlock's affliction. With only a few noted exceptions, the silver screen vampire will always be a predator at heart, regardless of his or her beliefs or revulsions, and that is clearly demonstrated in *Nosferatu*.

DEATH BE NOT PROUD

Count Orlock is significant on many levels, one of which is that he represents the scorned of society—a vile creature locked away in a remote run-down Transylvanian castle. Orlock eventually travels to Bremen to take up residence across the street from the traumatized Hutter and his high-strung, somnambulistic wife, Ellen.

Behind the entire real estate transaction is Hutter's boss, Knock (aka Renfield), who's under Orlock's spell and spends the film twirling about the village like a caffeinated lunatic who's downed one too many cases of Red Bull. What comes to pass at the film's apex is an interesting twist. Reading *The Book of the Vampires*, Ellen learns what she must do to save her beloved husband and destroy Orlock.

Willing the vampire to her bedroom, she offers herself to him as a blood sacrifice with the intention of keeping him busy until cock's crow. She succeeds, and as the sun rises and beams through the window, Orlock simply dissolves into a wisp of nothingness. Ellen, drained of her blood, has a final embrace with Hutter before dying. Given that most lead female victims of *Dracula* typically revert to humans upon the vampire's death, Ellen's heroic and selfless death is a dandy twist.

Enter Dracula, Stage Right

What may come as a surprise to you is that the first adaptation of Bram Stoker's novel was brought to the stage very quickly

after *Dracula*'s 1897 publication. The playwright was none other than Stoker himself and sadly, the play was a dismal failure,
in part because it was so difficult to present the proper ambi-
ence it so desperately required.

So bad was the production that it was said that even Stoker's close friend Henry Irving couldn't recommend it (see
Chapter 2). It wasn't until fellow Irishman Hamilton Deane,
himself a theater producer, playwright, and actor, decided to
take on the daunting project that *Dracula* would find its first
financial success.

In 1924, with the permission of Florence Stoker, Deane
debuted *Dracula* in Derby, England, at the Grand Theater.
The play starred Edmund Blake as the Count and Deane as
Dr. Van Helsing. And while critics of the day weren't necessarily kind, it was of little matter. Audiences loved it—and so
did Florence Stoker. That first appearance of Dracula onstage
is important, as it marks his first transformation as a proper
gentleman of royal blood who obviously possesses the mortal grace to interact with his victims, and *not* the fiend that
Stoker described in Jonathan Harker's journal in Chapter Two
of *Dracula*:

> "*His face was a strong, a very strong, aquiline, with
> high bridge of the thin nose and peculiarly arched nostrils,
> with lofty domed forehead, and hair growing scantily
> round the temples but profusely elsewhere. His eyebrows
> were very massive, almost meeting over the nose, and with
> bushy hair that seemed to curl in its own profusion. The
> mouth, so far as I could see it under the heavy moustache,
> was fixed and rather cruel-looking, with peculiarly sharp
> white teeth. These protruded over the lips, whose remark-
> able ruddiness showed astonishing vitality in a man of
> his years. For the rest, his ears were pale, and at the tops
> extremely pointed. The chin was broad and strong, and
> the cheeks firm though thin. The general effect was one of
> extraordinary pallor.*"

In 1927, Deane brought his production to London (this time
with Raymond Huntley in the lead role) where it again suf-

fered critical disdain but rated high with audiences who kept the play sold out for over five months. It was at that point that Horace Liveright, an American stage producer, purchased the rights to the play in order to bring *Dracula* to Broadway. To further rework and add to Deane's adaptation, American journalist John L. Balderston was hired by Liveright. In his version, Balderston made a number of adjustments, including merging Mina's character into Lucy's and further making Lucy the daughter of Dr. Seward.

The play premiered in October of 1927 at New York's Fulton Theater. This time the production starred a relatively unknown Hungarian actor named Bela Lugosi, who it was said was so obsessed with playing Dracula in the film version that he served as a mediator for Florence Stoker in negotiating the rights with Universal Pictures. He would, of course, go on to play Dracula in Tod Browning's 1931 feature-length film where he agreed to a nominal fee to play the Count, receiving a paltry $500 a week for the seven-week production.

Now you might be asking yourself why a stage play is so crucial to the vampire realm. What's so important about the Deane and Balderston renditions of *Dracula* is that their revamping of the Count in regard to physical appearance and also to Stoker's story line and characters set a precedent for many successful cinematic works to come, such as Lugosi's *Dracula* and the vampire in general.

The very idea that Dracula was a preternatural malfeasant who could appear as a cultured, domesticated human is in many ways far more frightening than his being a monstrous bloodthirsty savage. Ultimately, it was Deane's and Balderston's creative transformations that helped create the screen-savvy vampire we know today, one that audiences across the decades can relate to.

HAMMERING OUT HORROR

During the thirties and forties, Universal Pictures dominated the horror front beginning with Lugosi's *Dracula* and continuing with films like *Dracula's Daughter, Son of Dracula, House of Frankenstein,* and *House of Dracula.* But by the late 1950s, there came a re-emergence of the vampire film in the form of gothic horror, and on that front there was but one name—Hammer.

To fully understand the evolution of horror films and in particular the vampire genre, one must acknowledge the fine works of England's Hammer Films, whose contribution to the world of horror is nothing less than legendary.

It all began in 1913 when in Hammersmith, London, Enrique Carreras purchased his first in a line of cinemas. Three years later, he partnered with William Hind and together in 1934 they formed Hammer Productions, and a year later, Exclusive Films Ltd. as a distribution company. They immediately began making films, but were halted by the onset of World War II and couldn't continue distributing productions through Exclusive until 1945. Two years later, Hammer was revived and in 1949 became Hammer Film Productions Limited.

What happened in 1957 was Hammer's turning point, when they unleashed director Terence Fisher's *The Curse of Frankenstein* (based on the Mary Shelley novel *Frankenstein*), featuring Peter Cushing as Baron von Frankenstein and Christopher Lee as the creature.

The following year, the same trio teamed up for *Horror of Dracula,* which proved to be just the vehicle Hammer needed to solidify their status as the premiere horror film producers of the day. Both films were incredibly successful and would provide a starting point for a number of sequels and successive films.

Horror of Dracula in particular is said to have raked in over eight times the cost of the film's production. All the better that *Horror* and the Hammer Films to come were in color, adding to the visual appeal of the set designs and, of course, the blood. The film also marked the collaboration of director Fisher, writer Jimmy Sangster, and the duo who are without a doubt the most legendary pair in horror history—Christopher Lee and Peter Cushing (see Chapter 8).

HEART-POUNDING HORROR

The 1960s would prove to be an interesting decade for Hammer Films. While the 1960 *The Brides of Dracula* was one of Hammer's most popular in their vampire franchise, there's often a mixed cauldron of reviews for the film, which took the bold step of presenting viewers with a young blonde vampire called the Baron Meinster (played by David Peel). No doubt a Dracula flick without the tall, dark, and dangerous presence of Christopher Lee was a risk to be certain, but Peel, despite his youthful good looks, seemed to elicit mixed emotions both with critics and audiences. Folks loved him or hated him.

A trio of other vampire films would follow *Brides*, including *Kiss of the Vampire* (1964), which featured Hammer's first female vampire in Noel Willman, *Dracula: Prince of Darkness* (1966), and *Dracula Has Risen From the Grave* (1968). *Prince of Darkness* marked Christopher Lee's long-awaited return to the role he made famous, having intentionally stayed clear of the Dracula roles with the intent of avoiding being typecast.

Rumor has it that Lee was displeased with the script for *Dracula: Prince of Darkness* and insisting the dialog was atrocious, he refused to speak any of the lines. Apparently, Lee won out. In what amounted to a nonspeaking, mostly hissing and staring role, Lee again teamed with director Terence Fisher and writer Jimmy Sangster, and channeled his inner brute to terrorize two couples who happened upon his castle. Dracula indeed met his inevitable demise in the climax of the film, this time in icy waters.

Employing the intentional plotline succession from the end of one Dracula film to the beginning of the next, Lee's fiend was unintentionally revived in *Dracula Has Risen From the Grave* by a priest who himself plunged into the water, his blood reawakening the black devil. Without the direction of Terence Fisher, *Risen* lost the distinct romantic aspect so prevalent in the earlier Lee installments, instead favoring more action sequences.

THE NAIL IN THE COFFIN

Though the subject is often debated, part of Hammer's success in their Dracula productions was not mass-producing them. Eight years had passed from the time Christopher Lee first appeared in *Horror of Dracula* until he returned in *Dracula: Prince of Darkness*. By the 1970s, with pressure to create more revenue, the Dracula franchise inevitably suffered with one vampire flick coming after the other. Sadly, that strategy would work to Hammer's detriment and bring an end to their domination of the horror genre.

Hammer's first vampiric offering in the seventies was the 1970 film, *Taste the Blood of Dracula*. Again starring Lee, this installment saw his big bad bloodsucking self yet again resurrected, this time by Lord Courtley, who procured the Count's ring, his cloak, and a vial of blood. Later that year, Lee reprised his role in *Scars of Dracula*. Again resurrected with the help of a bat dripping blood on his immortal ashes, a rather sadistic Dracula torments a village until at last being struck by lightning.

Also released in 1970 was Hammer's *The Vampire Lovers*, featuring Ingrid Pitt in a surreal and exotic tale loosely based on Sheridan Le Fanu's "Carmilla" (see Chapter 2). The next year featured Pitt as *Countess Dracula*, followed by *Lust for a Vampire* (the sequel to *The Vampire Lovers*), directed by Jimmy Sangster.

In 1971, Peter Cushing attempted to squash the evils of vampirism in *Twins of Evil*, which again made use of Le Fanu's "Carmilla" characters. Then in 1972 came *Vampire Circus*, in which a vampire seeks revenge upon a plague-ridden village; and the sixth Christopher Lee performance in *Dracula A.D. 1972*, a more contemporary outing that reunited Lee with Cushing as his interminable foe, Dr. Abraham Van Helsing. Taking place in twentieth century London, the film also introduced Van Helsing's granddaughter, Jessica, who would also take part in Lee's final Dracula film, *Satanic Rites of Dracula* in 1974, which sadly marked his final vampiric pairing with Cushing.

After *Satanic Rites,* Lee bid adieu to his most famous Hammer alter ego, one of the most famous and historic portrayals in vampire cinematic history. Following the release of *Captain Kronos: Vampire Hunter* in 1974 (see Chapter 10), Hammer Films, acquiescing to the realization that gothic horror had run its course, ceased its productions of vampire cinema, ending a legacy and leaving filmmakers of the future to create new and imaginative versions of the vampire of the ages.

And just to show how much impact the Hammer films truly had, it must be mentioned that the cloak Lee originally wore during *Horror of Dracula* was found in October of 2007 in a London dress shop. Missing for three decades, the cape, which was verified by Lee himself as the original, is valued at upwards of $44,000.

Goiπg Batty for Bad Boys!

What would take place from the mid-1970s to the present-day, with the precedents set by the film *Nosferatu,* the stage adaptations written by Hamilton Deane and John Balderston, and Hammer Films, was the opening of a mausoleum bursting with various plotlines, creative license, and the benefits of technical advancements just waiting to be employed. And best of all— some of the most legendary vampire portrayals in history.

Chapter 8

LEGENDARY BLOOD DRINKERS

Now that you've explored the birth of the cinematic vampire, it's time to get to the actors and actresses who have, over the decades, given us a bloody good show by donning fangs, capes, and major attitude. Do you have a favorite cinematic sucker? Indeed, there are a coffin-full of performances and films worth noting for the characters and story lines they bring to life and the immortality they bring to the horror genre. This includes a host of blood drinkers, like Bela Lugosi, Christopher Lee, Gary Oldman, and Kate Beckinsale, who most would readily agree are Grade A, or shall we say, the Type A of cinematic vampire consumption. Pun intended.

I *Vant* to Suck Your Blood!

Since the inception of vampiric cinema, dozens of actors and actresses have taken on the challenge of playing the most famous bloodsuckers in history. Some, like Bela Lugosi, Christopher Lee, Frank Langella, Catherine Deneuve, Kate Beckinsale, and Gary Oldman to name a few, have left a permanent bite on the genre. Others failed to achieve the same critical acclaim. But it's fair to say that playing a character so embedded in lore, literature, and film is no easy stroll through the cemetery.

If you're like most folks, selecting your favorite Dracula is akin to choosing your favorite James Bond. Some folks prefer the almost balletic and traditional performance of Lugosi, while others lean toward Christopher Lee's seductive but utterly ruthless Dracula. Still others prefer Max Schreck's Count Orlock, who by whatever magic of lighting, makeup, or our own imaginations, becomes more grotesque and repugnant as the film *Nosferatu* progresses.

In the modern era, with the growing sophistication of computer graphics, makeup techniques, and creative camera work, horror fans have the benefit of being treated to more upscale bloodsuckers such as Oldman's seamless vampiric changing from young man to old and then into rats and wolves.

Still others would prefer Frank Langella, Willem Dafoe, Stuart Townsend, John Carradine, Jonathan Frid, Barbara Steele, George Hamilton, or any number of thespians who grabbed a set of sharp canines and took their best shot at proclaiming: "I never drink . . . wine." Or in the case of Gerard Butler in *Dracula 2000*, the very modernized: "I never drink . . . coffee."

For sheer artistry and panache, it must be said that every actor and actress who's portrayed a vampire has brought some measure of charm and idiosyncrasy to their undead alter egos, and *all* of their portrayals—the good, the bad, and the ugly—have added another crystal to the kaleidoscope of silver screen vampirism. Let's focus then, on some of the most famous of the silver screen suckers, beginning with Bela Lugosi.

BELA LUGOSI

In 1931, in what many consider to be one of the greatest, if not *the* greatest vampire film of all time, actor Bela Lugosi introduced the public to Count Dracula in the first official version based on Bram Stoker's novel. For Lugosi, it's arguably the role of a lifetime, one that secured his legacy in the kingdom of silver screen horror and one that was a long time in the making.

Given the ferocity with which Stoker's widow, Florence Stoker, fought to have the 1922 "unauthorized" film *Nosferatu* literally destroyed, it's a miracle the rights to Stoker's novel were finally secured when Florence sold them to Universal Pictures (see Chapter 7). With his Hungarian accent and the constant light beaming from his eyes, Lugosi set in stone the menace, obsession, charm, and depravity we've come to expect of the most wicked denizen of the night. Many of Dracula's famous lines and powers appeared in the 1931 version, and were readily mimicked or enhanced in many future vampire films.

Director Tod Browning's interpretation, which was actually based more on the Deane and Balderston stage production of *Dracula* (see Chapter 7) drew elements from Stoker's novel, but also took creative license with its characters and progression. For example, in Browning's depiction, it's Renfield who takes center stage rather than the relatively downplayed "John" Harker.

Despite it being a low-budget production, *Dracula* was Universal Pictures' highest grossing film of 1931. Released on Valentine's Day weekend, which happened to be Friday the thirteenth, rumor has it that women were fainting in the theater aisles and that men were running from the building! In a final tribute to his legendary portrayal, Lugosi, who died on August 16, 1956, was buried in his Dracula costume.

CHRISTOPHER LEE

For many vampire aficionados, the bloodsucking buck stops with legendary actor Christopher Lee. With over 260 films to his credit since 1948, Lee is one of this generation's most talented and prolific actors and one of the greatest stars in horror history. During his epic career, which shows no signs of slowing, Lee has played Dracula, Frankenstein, the Mummy, Sherlock Holmes, Fu Manchu, and scores of villainous performances from Rasputin to Francisco Scaramanga in *The Man with the Golden Gun.*

Most recently, he played Saruman in the *Lord of the Rings* trilogy, and Count Dooku in the *Star Wars* episodes *Revenge of the Sith* and *Attack of the Clones.* And get this—Lee is cited in the *Guinness Book of World Records* as holding the record for being the actor who's appeared in the most sword-fight scenes in cinematic history. It wasn't until the 2002 film *Star Wars II: Attack of the Clones* that Lee, at the age of eighty, ceased performing his own stunt work.

Lee ended up playing Dracula over seventeen times in his career, with seven of those portrayals done for Hammer Films including *Horror of Dracula, Dracula: Prince of Darkness, Dracula Has Risen from the Grave, Taste the Blood of Dracula, Scars of Dracula, Dracula A.D. 1972,* and *Satanic Rites of Dracula.*

What ultimately makes Lee one of the most—if not the most—popular cinematic sucker in history is the amalgam of traits he brought to the character. At six-foot-five, his tall, dark, and exotically handsome looks, coupled with his trademark intensity gave Lee the freedom to build his Dracula into not only an animalistic predator, but a shrewd and seductive bad boy.

Having played the fiend more than any other actor, Lee, whether he was fighting Van Helsing or securing his latest female conquest, proved to the world that his calculating creature bore the intellect, cunning, and seductive appeal to which all future Draculas could only hope to aspire.

PETER CUSHING

Though he typically played superlative vampire hunter Abraham Van Helsing, it would be woefully inappropriate to exclude Peter Cushing from a discussion of legendary vampire performers, especially given his longstanding screen partnership and lifelong friendship with Christopher Lee.

Few acting partnerships are the stuff legends are made of, and in the horror realm there is but one duo—Cushing and Lee. They made nineteen films together, but are perhaps best known for their vampire cinema.

An impeccably mannered British gent with piercing blue eyes, Cushing—no matter his role—made you feel safe and protected, and in the vampire realm, that's a tall order. In truth, more often than not, it was Cushing's Van Helsing who carried the Dracula films, with Lee concentrating his efforts on his bloodthirsty physical intimidation rather than words.

Part of what sets Cushing apart from the previous incarnations of Van Helsing, Edward Van Sloan in particular (who played the doctor in both the 1931 *Dracula* and the 1936 sequel *Dracula's Daughter*), is that not only was he the perfect combination of gentle but obsessed intellect, he brought to the character a physical presence.

Agile and athletic, Cushing was typically the only voice of reason in the Dracula films, and as such, was usually the one person who could lay waste to the bloodsucker du jour. In doing so, he would go to great lengths to tussle with the black devil, on many an occasion even being bitten himself.

Throughout his distinguished career from 1939 to 1986, Cushing was a consummate pro who played everything from Dr. Frankenstein, to Sherlock Holmes, to Dr. Who, and Grand Moff Tarkin in *Star Wars*. His passing in 1994 is something Christopher Lee still mourns, saying he never felt as open with or as close with any of his friends as he did Cushing.

GARY OLDMAN

In the annals of Dracula legend, Gary Oldman is arguably one of the all-time best interpreters of the Count, if for no other reason than that his portrayal of the ancient bloodsucker is a tour de force of emotions one would expect—but are not always entirely shown—from a predator eternally consumed by anger, revenge, lust, love, and power. His brilliant performance in

Francis Ford Coppola's 1992 *Bram Stoker's Dracula* shows us in no uncertain terms the extent to which Dracula will go to remedy what is at best a tragic love tale gone horribly wrong. As far as vampire films are concerned, Coppola's version is without question one of the best ever made, from its stylish aura to its stellar cast.

What makes Oldman's performance so extraordinary in this gothic, romantic horrorfest is how seamlessly he shifts from deranged old vampire to handsome young Prince Vlad to various incarnations of wolf and bat and grotesque fanged monster of folklore.

As did his accomplished vampiric predecessors, Oldman does well to show the core existence of the ultimate bad boy, with an accelerated sense of intense charm and intelligence that tautly belies his extreme depravity. His ability to convey the overwhelming loneliness of immortality elicits an empathy rarely captured in vampire cinema.

Opting to forgo CGI technology, Coppola insisted that the special effects be accomplished using camera trickery, with clever use of camera angles and "old school" techniques which proved admirably successful. At its core, the script attempts to retain the best parts of Stoker's original work and greatly benefits not only from Oldman, but Sir Anthony Hopkins, who must be duly noted as being one of the best actors to ever take on the daunting role of Abraham Van Helsing.

The Vampire Hall of Fame

Since the creation of film, dozens of actors and actresses have played vampires. While there are a few who stand fang and cape above the rest, there are several other notable performances that must be mentioned.

In particular, the 1973 American made-for-television production of *Dracula* starring renowned character actor Jack Palance, who with Frank Langella and his 1979 performance triggered a resurgence of Dracula popularity. Well suited to the role with his intimidating physique, distinguished demeanor, and menacing voice, Palance breathed new life into the immortal bad boy, benefiting from a script written by *I Am Legend* author Richard Matheson and *Dark Shadows* director Dan Curtis.

FRANK LANGELLA

Starring as Dracula in the 1979 version, Frank Langella is considered by many to be one of the finest actors to play the role. Supremely indulgent in its Edwardian setting and graced with Sir Laurence Olivier as Van Helsing and Donald Pleasence as Dr. Seward, Langella's fiend is the epitome of charm, seduction, and demonic manipulation. Based on the Deane and Balterston stage play (see Chapter 7), it is at times almost campy in its efforts to revive Lugosi's original *Dracula* but with a decidedly modern edge meant to keep female audience members in a hypnotic swoon. If you're looking for a vampiric hottie—Langella's your guy!

JOHN CARRADINE

Easily one of history's most prolific actors, the patriarch of the Carradine family played Dracula on numerous occasions (second only to Christopher Lee) on the stage and both big and small screens, most notably during the 1940s in *House of Frankenstein* and *House of Dracula*.

In 1956, he had the distinction of playing the first television Dracula in an episode of *Matinee Theatre*. He then went on to portray the bloodsucker in the comedies *Billy the Kid versus Dracula* (1966) and *Nocturna* (1979), also known as *Granddaughter of Dracula*, while also appearing in a number of campy vamp flicks. Suffice to say, that in the vampire hall of fame—John Carradine is one of the creepiest.

JONATHAN FRID

In his portrayal of Barnabas Collins in the landmark gothic daytime soap opera *Dark Shadows*, Jonathan Frid saved the program from imminent cancellation by showing us the multidimensional—if not campy—side of a vampire torn apart by reluctance and primal urges (see Chapter 11).

The first serious television bloodsucker, Barnabas Collins was originally conceived as part of a temporary subplot, but his instant popularity guaranteed a lasting position as one of the show's protagonists—a role that led to two feature-length films, and many thousands of die-hard fans who remain devoted to this day. Frid maintains his own Web site at *www.jonathanfrid.com*, and regularly responds to comments from his adoring fans.

WILLEM DAFOE

It's a rare occurrence when a horror or sci-fi star receives an Oscar nod, which tells you just how amazing Willem Dafoe's performance was in the 2000 film *Shadow of the Vampire*, which portrayed the making of the 1922 film *Nosferatu* (see Chapter 7). Portraying actor Max Schreck, Dafoe showed a depth of introspective depravity rarely seen in vampire cinema, one that played well to the film's ultimate twist—that F.W. Murnau's obsession to cast his "perfect" vampire leads to the ominous conclusion that perhaps Schreck so perfectly played a vampire because he *was* a vampire. Now *there's* a spooky thought!

TOM CRUISE AND BRAD PITT

In 1994, the long-awaited adaptation of Anne Rice's *Interview with the Vampire: The Vampire Chronicles* at last came to fruition. It was a lavish period production, but there appears to be little gray area in regard to audience reception—people love it or revile it, with opponents citing Neil Jordan's ultimate casting of Cruise and Pitt as a calculated effort to entice the teenage contingent. Regardless, *Interview*, which ranks third among the all-time grossing vampire films, remains true to the novel and is proficient in relating the eternal drama of the charming, complex, and magnetic Lestat de Lioncourt and his reluctant fledgling Louis de Pointe du Lac (see Chapters 6 and 10).

STUART TOWNSEND

Based on Anne Rice's *Vampire Chronicles* (a combination of *The Vampire Lestat* and *The Queen of the Damned*), the 2002 *Queen of the Damned* gave us our second glimpse of the most famous vampire since Stoker's Dracula (see Chapter 6).

Taking on the highly revered Lestat for this adaptation is Stuart Townsend, who on many levels does due justice to the sheer complexity of a vampire whose journey in this installment takes him from his awakening as a rock star to destroyer of Akasha, the ancient mother of all vampires. What Cruise lacks in depth, the smoldering Townsend finds in his goth arrogance and willingness to ire every vampire on Earth by doing the unthinkable and breaking the code of anonymity.

RICHARD ROXBURGH

As the second highest grossing vampire film of all time, the 2004 film *Van Helsing* has much to offer in its action-packed Transylvanian travail, not the least of which is a stellar performance by Aussie actor Richard Roxburgh. Fighting his mortal—or immortal foe in this case—Gabriel Van Helsing, Roxburgh is arguably one of the best Draculas we've seen in years.

Frightening in his emotional depravity, and utterly manipulative, Roxburgh's evil demon is driven to the point of frenzy in his goal of unleashing his progeny on the world while also playing a wicked hide-and-go-bite with Van Helsing in an epic battle of bat versus werewolf (see Chapter 10).

WESLEY SNIPES

Born of a mother who was bitten by a vampire just prior to his birth, Wesley Snipes as Blade brings a new dimension to the vampire realm. Not only is he half human, half bloodsucker—he's a vampire hunter. Born of Marvel Comics in their 1973 offering *The Tomb of Dracula*, Blade has the distinct advantage of being a "daywalker," meaning he has no aversion to sunlight and relatively few of the vulnerabilities suffered by the typical vampire (see Chapter 10). Packed with action, the *Blade* trilogy ultimately epitomizes the reluctant vampire. Blade doesn't feed on humans or animals, instead using various injectables to quench his thirst.

GERARD BUTLER

In Wes Craven's *Dracula 2000*, Gerard Butler takes his turn as the ultimate bad boy. In a very modern tale with a truly inspired plot, Butler's Dracula goes neck-to-neck with both Van Helsing and his unwary daughter, Mary. Unlike the bloodsuckers of old who are typically descended from Stoker's amalgam of Vlad the Impaler and his father Vlad Dracul, Craven chose to link his vampire to a biblical source, namely Judas Iscariot—the betrayer of Christ. With several excellent twists and turns, *Dracula 2000* is one of the better vampire films of the modern era (see Chapter 5).

WILLIAM MARSHALL

The precursor to Wesley Snipes's African American vampire was a man by the name of Prince Mamuwalde, played by William Marshall, who made the grave mistake of attempting to deal with Dracula during the late 1700s in regard to banishing the slave trade. Bad idea. Mamuwalde wakes up in 1972 only to realize he's become Blacula. A quintessential seventies vamp flick, it's no mystery that *Blacula* came on the heels of the Civil Rights movement, but Marshall deserves props for playing the somewhat campy vamp with dignity, panache, and a rugged charm that led to the sequel *Scream Blacula Scream* in 1973.

ANDERS HOVE

Though it's often classified as a B-movie for its direct-to-video releases, the *Subspecies* series is unique in its willingness to forgo the traditional debonair Dracula in favor of one more typical of folkloric vampires and *Nosferatu's* heinous Count Orlock. Anders Hove's portrayal of the ghoulish Romanian vampire Radu Vladislaus, with his huge fangs, drippy drool, mutant features, and raspy voice, is *truly* the stuff nightmares are made of. Definitely not your kiss-and-bite hunky be-my-valentine vamp.

Here Come the Brides!

Until the onset of the modern era of vampire cinema, most females were often relegated to portraying Dracula's brides, typically chosen from a contingent of barmaids, peasants, travelers, or various amalgams of Stoker's Lucy Westenra or Mina Murray (see Chapter 2). In the usual Dracula format, one or more of these women perish either due to having been bitten or at the hands of a vampire hunter, with the last bride's vampiric condition often reversed with Dracula's demise. But over the years, a small brood of leading actresses crept from their coffins to begin the evolution of the female vampire as a legitimate dyed-in-the-cape threat.

Early Vixens of Vampirism

One of the first of the silver screen vamps is Gloria Holden, who captured the lead in the 1936 *Dracula's Daughter,* a sequel to Lugosi's *Dracula* (see Chapter 9). As Countess Marya Zaleska, Holden gives an icy and hypnotic portrayal that's not without its manipulative charms. Contrary to the action-oriented female vampires of the modern era, the Countess is a reluctant vampire longing to find a cure for her evil affliction. At its core, Holden's portrayal put the cinematic world on notice that female vampires—with their own seductive ploys and predatory capacities—were on the hunt.

MARIA MENADO

During the 1950s, several more female vampires crawled out of their coffins. Rarely mentioned as a leading lady vampire, most likely due to the fact that the film wasn't widely released in the United States is Maria Menado, who in 1957 played the vampire antagonist in a pair of Malaysian films called *Pontianak* (*The Vampire*) and *Dendam Pontianak* (*Revenge of the Vampire*), based on the Malaysian revenant of folklore (see Chapter 1). Given the fact that vengeful bloodsuckers are tricky to kill and fast to reanimate, Menado arose from the dead again in 1958 in *Sumpah Pontianak* (*The Vampire's Curse*), and *Pontianak Kembali* (*The Vampire Returns*) in 1963.

BARBARA STEELE

During the 1960s, Italian director Mario Bava produced a number of classic horror films including *Black Sabbath*, *Planet of the Vampires*, and *Hercules vs. the Vampires*, but it was his 1960 cult classic *La Maschera del demonio*, commonly known as *Black Sunday* that turned the tide of Italian vampire cinema. It was on the set of the 1956 film *I Vampiri* (aka *The Devil's Commandment*) that cinematographer turned director Mario Bava realized the horror potential of a strikingly beautiful brunette actress named Barbara Steele. Playing the dual role of Princess Asa Vajda and Katia Vajda, Steele gives a spectacular performance as a seventeenth century vampiric witch and the virgin Katia in what is a stylish, romantic, and seductive feast of chilling vampiric horror.

INGRID PITT

During the 1970s, Hammer Films came out with a trilogy of highly successful and boldly seductive films based on Sheridan Le Fanu's "Carmilla," including *The Vampire Lovers*, *Lust for a Vampire*, and *Twins of Evil*. The first of the three launched the horror career of Polish-born beauty Ingrid Pitt. As the vampire Mircalla/Carmilla in *Vampire Lovers*, Pitt proved herself to be a formidable bloodsucker who turns a trio of her own brides in the ultimate female power play.

Pitt continued padding her vampiric acting resume by playing the lead in the 1971 film *Countess Dracula*, and that same year fanged-up for *The House that Dripped Blood*, a somewhat comedic horror anthology in which she starred in an episode entitled "The Cloak."

BLOODTHIRSTY BABES

After the exotic vampires of the seventies, the next three decades introduced us to a number of naughty vampiric vixens who ran the gamut from dramatic to comedic to otherworldly. Among them were Louise Fletcher in *Mama Dracula* (1980), Mathilda May in *Lifeforce* (1985), Lauren Hutton in *Once Bitten* (1985), Grace Jones in *Vamp* (1986), Britt Ekland in *Beverly Hills Vamp* (1989), Sylvia Kristel in *Dracula's Widow* (1989), Anna Parillaud in *Innocent Blood* (1992), Talisa Soto in *Vampirella* (1996), Denice Duff in the *Subspecies* series, Kristanna Loken as the hybrid human-dhampir in *BloodRayne* (2005), and Lucy Liu in *Rise* (2007).

All of these characters brought to the genre a new breed of female fiend that would set in motion the idea that women could carry a vampire film. Among them, however, a few blood-sucking beauties give particularly remarkable performances. The first of these is one of vampire cinema's most renowned immortals—Catherine Deneuve.

CATHERINE DENEUVE

France's Catherine Deneuve is arguably one of the best actresses of her time, beginning with one of her earliest major roles in Roman Polanski's 1965 *Repulsion* to the 1967 tour de force performance in *Belle du jour* to her 1992 Oscar-nominated Best Actress performance in *Indochine*. But in 1983, Deneuve transformed into a sensuous creature of a different kind when she became Miriam Blaylock, the several millennia old vampire in *The Hunger*, adapted from the 1981 Whitley Strieber novel of the same name (see Chapter 6).

As with all novel-to-film adaptations, there are noted differences in plot (especially the film's ending), but what sets *The Hunger* apart from other films of the genre is the stylish upper-crust look created by director Tony Scott (who went on to direct *Top Gun* and *Days of Thunder* among others).

The film was largely criticized for its primary focus on visual appeal, but ultimately there's little to dislike about Deneuve's cold and calculated vampiric portrayal. With a torrid mix of decadence and predatorial ferocity, Miriam is a classy but subliminally terrifying vampire whose intimidation offers a glimpse into the ruthless psyche of an ancient immortal.

Also starring David Bowie as her "dying" lover and Susan Sarandon as Miriam's chosen replacement, the cult classic is most commonly noted for its tasteful scenes between Deneuve and Sarandon.

KATE BECKINSALE

With the onset of successful literary adaptations including Coppola's *Bram Stoker's Dracula* in 1992, followed by Anne Rice's *Interview with the Vampire* and *Queen of the Damned*, and the ongoing *Blade* series, the world of vampire cinema was searching for fresh female blood, especially of the action-oriented type.

What they found was Kate Beckinsale, cast in the lead role of Selene in the 2003 film *Underworld* and its sequel, *Underworld: Evolution* in 2006 (see Chapter 10). If you're keen on Greek mythology, then you'll be interested to know that Selene is the goddess of the moon in all its phases, representing the fullness of life.

More than just your average run-of-the-mill bloodsucking vixen, Selene epitomizes a new-age girl power, casting herself smack in the middle of a deadly war being fought for the better part of a millennium between vampires and lycans (arguably the best werewolves you'll *ever* see transform on the big screen).

Selene's smoldering sensuality plays in brilliant contrast to her extreme survival instinct as a "death dealer" and the tumultuous risks she takes in the name of revenge, regardless of the laws of her coven. Also intermingled in the bloody savoir faire is the introduction of a male protagonist, Michael, who in his fight against becoming a hybrid, stirs in Selene the memories of what it was once like to be human.

While the sequel, which takes up where its predecessor ends, doesn't quite hold the same serum as the original, it does serve to further establish that there's nothing sexier than a female vamp in skintight leather—especially one who knows right from wrong and can play the undead game from hilt to blade.

The *Underworld* flicks proved successful enough to bring viewers to the 2006 film *Ultraviolet,* where a seriously pumped-up vampiric plague sufferer, brilliantly played by Milla Jovovich, wreaks major havoc in a futuristic society hellbent on eliminating her "kind" (see Chapter 10).

Fun with Vampirism

As with all movie genres, there exist films that, while the intent was to provide serious drama and suspense, the ultimate product proved to be unintentionally humorous. Thankfully, there are a few vampire comedies, spoofs, and parodies that serve to lighten the mood of the terminally dark critters of the night.

Over the decades, many filmmakers have made attempts at vampire comedy, including *Tempi duri per i vampiri,* aka *Hard Times for Dracula (1959), The Fearless Vampire Killers* (1967), *Andy Warhol's Dracula* (1974), *Vampira* (1974), *Once Bitten* (1985), *I Married a Vampire* (1987), *My Grandfather Is a Vampire* (1991), *Innocent Blood* (1992), and *Vampire in Brooklyn* (1995), to name a few.

Arguably the most successful of the vampire comedy/spoofs that enjoy longevity is the 1992 film *Buffy the Vampire Slayer,* which became a long-running television series, beginning in 1997.

Comedy and spoof filmmakers of the modern vampire genre take on a major challenge, because in truth, they're held up to the high standard set by what's considered by many to be the ultimate horror spoof—director Mel Brooks' 1974 classic *Young Frankenstein.*

In 1995, Brooks again ventured into the genre with the spoof *Dracula: Dead and Loving It,* starring Leslie Nielsen as the bumbling bloodsucker, a brilliantly insane Peter Mac-Nichol as Renfield, and an admirable group of comedians, including Harvey Korman (Dr. Seward), Steven Weber (Jonathan Harker), Amy Yasbeck (Mina), and Mel Brooks himself as Van Helsing.

Amid the comedic vampire genre, however, there's one offering that many consider to be the definitive classic of the genre, and that came in the form of perpetually tanned actor George Hamilton. The film is *Love at First Bite*, and as a parody, the 1979 film really was tailor-made for the tall, dashing, debonair Hamilton, who posed little threat to classic Draculas by giving an over-the-top performance as an ages-old nosferatu who attempts to blend into modern-day New York City.

Bite made a strong attempt at updating the vampire films of old by employing a distinctly modern edge. For example, when Dracula's told that he can spend the rest of his life in an efficiency apartment with seven dissidents and a single toilet, he asks Renfield: "What is an efficiency apartment?" To which Renfield (played by comedian Arte Johnson) replies: "What's a toilet?"

As far as legendary Dracula dialog, it's likely few fans of the vampire genre will forget Hamilton's heavily accented classic lines, including "Children of the night . . . shut up!" or "How would you like to be dressed as a head waiter for the last 700 years?"

Hemoglobin Heaven

So, now that you've gained insight into a few of the most bitingly renowned bad boys and girls of the silver screen, who's your favorite? As mentioned at the start of this chapter, choosing a favorite vampire is no easy feat. Fortunately, you can now indulge in an easy way to pick a few flicks featuring a wide range of cinematic bloodsuckers by delving into a two-part filmography that will no doubt enhance your mortal love of all things, well . . . immortal!

Chapter 9

Reel-Time: The Silent Era Through the Swinging Sixties

For more than a century, the movie-making industry has produced all manner of films in the horror genre, and a large and historically significant part of that body of work are films focused on vampires. From the Silent Era to the present day, we've been treated to a variety of bloodsuckers, from the dramatic to the spooky to the downright comedic. No matter the decade, each of these films has made a contribution to vampire lore, paying homage to both the literary works they're based on and the creative minds who've conjured up some of the hippest, and most horrifying and engaging monsters the world has ever seen.

Silver Screen Suckers

Did you know that vampires and the subject of vampirism in its various incarnations have played an important role in horror history since the Silent Era? Fortunately for us vampire fanatics, the power of bloodsuckers shows no sign of fizzling into the sunrise any time in the foreseeable future.

While the horror genre has most certainly seen its share of B-movies and requisite fake blood, furry bats bopping up and down like yo-yos, and fangtastic dental work, there are plenty of early classics that in their simplicity make vampires convincingly real and utterly frightening. In truth, many of the vampire films of the mid-twentieth century have withstood the test of time, with a host of additional films becoming cult classics many years later. Even more compelling are the vampires of the modern era, where new breeds of bloodsuckers have emerged with stylish aplomb—and a whole lot of hemoglobin and bad attitude.

In perusing this two-part vampire filmography, you may be surprised by the wide range of story lines they follow, from those building off Bram Stoker's *Dracula*, to artistic spinoffs, action-adventure extravaganzas, foreign interpretations, and even a few prized spoofs for good measure.

For the purposes of this guide, a select group of films are highlighted to give you an inkling of the full range of creative efforts filmmakers have worked hard to present, from short silent films to formidable full-blown big-budget epics. No matter your vampiric preference, if you love nightcrawlers, then *all* of these flicks are worth sinking your teeth into. In this chapter, we focus on films from the Silent Era through the 1960s, while in Chapter 10 you can peruse films from the 1970s through the new millennium.

The Silent Era

You might think that silent films are boring. That's perfectly understandable. Some of them are. But bear in mind that silent films by their very nature are classics, and those in the horror genre are no exception. While the most recognizable of the silent vampire films is F. W. Murnau's 1922 film *Nosferatu* which you learned about in Chapter 7, there are dozens more that give audiences a glimpse into the true evolutionary beginnings of the cinematic vampire as well as the underpinnings of the political and societal constrictions and conflicts of the era.

Sadly, a fair number of these silent gems didn't survive the ravages of time, so their legacy, like so many Draculas, is turned to dust. *Nosferatu* as well as a few others however, are readily available and a must-see for all vampire fans.

Believe it or not, the first glimpse of vampirism saw the light of day in 1896 in a two-minute French film called *Le Manoir du diable*, or *Manor of the Devil*. Short but horrifyingly sweet, *Manoir* starred a bat which transformed itself into Mephistopheles. Despite being a short piece, the film is considered by many to be the first vampire film.

Several dozen more vamp flicks would follow over the next two decades, and their creation would reveal an interesting contrast between European and American filmmakers of the era, the Europeans choosing to focus more on artistic and expressionist movie-making, and the Americans beginning a trend of producing more action-oriented films.

One of the most noteworthy films of the Silent Era is director Tod Browning's 1927 horror mystery *London After Midnight*. Browning is one of the directors who crossed over from the silents to talkies, and is often considered to be one of America's premiere silent film directors.

Part of his success was his association with Lon Chaney Sr., who achieved acclaim for his 1923 portrayal of Quasimodo in *The Hunchback of Notre Dame*, and a number of other silent films that earned him the nickname the "Man of a Thousand Faces." As the star of *London After Midnight*, replete with a mouthful of sharp vampire teeth, bulging eyes and droopy eyelids, and stovepipe hat and vampire cloak, Chaney certainly lived up to his nickname.

Based on an original story written by Browning, *London After Midnight* is a Scotland Yard mystery, one that many experts playfully consider to be the first "fake" vampire film, given that Chaney serves double duty as both Inspector Burke and a mysterious vampiric character created as part of an elaborate deception to uncover a murderer. The film was remade by Browning in 1935 as *Mark of the Vampire* starring Lionel Barrymore and Bela Lugosi.

The 1930s: The Dawn of Dracula

While it's often debated as to which vampire film marks the actual "birth" of vampiric cinema, with many noting that *Nosferatu* is the first to follow—although without permission—Bram Stoker's *Dracula*, there really should be little dispute. The first official portrayal of the father of all immortal bad boys and his torrid Transylvanian tale falls to Bela Lugosi, who in 1931 brought the traditional Dracula to the screen with every ounce of preternatural panache he could muster (see Chapter 8).

Though many versions would follow over the decades, Lugosi's portrayal of Dracula is significant on many levels. It was indeed this film that introduced many of the bloodsucker's characteristics, including his ability to transform into bats, wolves, mist and dust, his aversion to mirrors, and the utterances of what have become trademark dialog for Dracula. No vampire fan will ever forget Lugosi's heavily accented and diabolical: "I never drink . . . wine."

The 1930s also saw the emergence of one of the most notable and somewhat underrated female vampires of the genre, Gloria Holden, who in 1936 flew onto the big screen in *Dracula's Daughter*. Picking up the story precisely where Lugosi's version ends, Holden, as the Countess Marya Zaleska, is one of the first in a long line of what would come to be known as reluctant vampires—one who seeks to break the curse of immortality.

Allegedly based on Bram Stoker's story "Dracula's Guest" (many experts cite the script as having actually been the original work of Garrett Fort, who also wrote the 1931 *Dracula*), this sequel is often overlooked. Despite its obvious low budget, however, it remains a stylish example that would only serve to help further the brood of female vampires to come (see Chapter 8). If you want to be mesmerized by one of the best ice maidens in the vampire realm, then definitely check out *Dracula's Daughter*.

Several other films of the thirties are worthy of note, the first of which is director Carl Theodor Dreyer's 1932 German offering *Vampyr*, a somewhat bizarre and cryptic tale based on Sheridan Le Fanu's "Carmilla" (see Chapter 2).

A year later, audiences were treated to *The Vampire Bat*, featuring Lionel Atwill, Fay Wray, a young Melvyn Douglas, and Dwight Frye, who gave a truly lunatic performance as Bela Lugosi's slave, Renfield, in the 1931 *Dracula*. And in 1935, came *Mark of the Vampire*, the remake of Tod Browning's *London After Midnight*.

Believe it or not, even Humphrey Bogart took his turn as a vampire-zombie in the 1939 flick *The Return of Dr. X*. Yep. Complete with white streak in his hair, Bogie portrays an executed murderer who's reanimated with the added benefits of vampirism. As a matter of curiosity, the role was originally meant for Boris Karloff.

A few of the more renowned flicks of the 1930s include:

- *Dracula* (1931) Bela Lugosi, Helen Chandler, David Manners, Edward Van Sloan
- *Drácula* (1931, Mexico) Carlos Villarías, Pablo Álvarez Rubio, Barry Norton, Lupita Tovar
- *Vampyr*, aka *Castle of Doom*, aka *Vampyr—Der Traum des Allan Grey*, aka *The Strange Adventure of David Gray* (1932, Germany) Julian West, Maurice Schutz, Rena Mandel
- *The Last Man on Earth*, aka *El Ultimo varon sobre la Tierra* (1933, Mexico) Raul Roulien, Rosita Moreno, Mimi Aguglia

THE GIRL'S GUIDE TO **Vampires**

- *The Vampire Bat* (1933) Lionel Atwill, Fay Wray, Melvyn Douglas
- *Mark of the Vampire* (1935) Lionel Barrymore, Elizabeth Allan, Bela Lugosi, Lionel Atwill
- *Dracula's Daughter* (1936) Otto Kruger, Gloria Holden, Marguerite Churchill
- *The Macabre Trunk*, aka *El Baúl macabro* (1936, Mexico) Ramón Pereda, René Cardona, Manuel Noriega
- *The Return of Dr. X* (1939) Humphrey Bogart, Rosemary Lane, Wayne Morris

THE 1940S: THE COMEDY OF HORROR

The onset of the 1940s saw the vampire genre endure a few wicked and amusing escapades (some not intentionally comedic), while also highlighting a few horror heavyweights who took their turn playing Dracula. Lugosi returned to the role in several films including *The Devil Bat, Spooks Run Wild, The Return of the Vampire*, and even played the bloodsucker in *Abbott and Costello Meet Frankenstein*.

Of these films, only *Return* gives Lugosi a role he can chomp into, playing Armand Tesla, a vampire who's initially destroyed in 1918, but uncovered and reanimated during World War II. Significantly, the film marks the first time a vampire meets the Wolf Man.

Also joining the crypt of the distinguished vampyr is Lon Chaney, as the mustached Count Alucard (*Dracula* spelled backwards) in *Son of Dracula*. Chaney had a busy decade, pulling triple monster duty as famed Wolf Man Lawrence Talbot in *Abbott and Costello Meet Frankenstein, House of Frankenstein*, and *House of Dracula*. It was, in fact, the latter two romps that introduced us to yet another legendary cinematic bloodsucker—John Carradine, who is arguably one of the creepiest of the classic Draculas (see Chapter 8).

A few of the more well known dramas and comedies of horrors from the 1940s include:

- *The Devil Bat* (1940) Bela Lugosi, Suzanne Kaaren, Dave O'Brien, Hal Price
- *Spooks Run Wild* (1941) Bela Lugosi, Leo Gorcey, Dennis Moore
- *Dr. Terror's House of Horrors* (1943) Henriette Gérard, Murdock MacQuarrie, Paul Wegener
- *Son of Dracula* (1943) Lon Chaney Jr., Robert Paige, Louise Allbritton, Evelyn Ankers
- *House of Frankenstein* (1944) John Carradine, Boris Karloff, Lon Chaney Jr., Lionel Atwill
- *The Return of the Vampire* (1944) Bela Lugosi, Matt Willis, Frieda Inescort, Nina Foch
- *House of Dracula* (1945) Lon Chaney Jr., John Carradine, Lionel Atwill,
- *Isle of the Dead* (1945) Boris Karloff, Ellen Drew, Marc Cramer
- *Memorias de una Vampiresa* (1945, Mexico) Manuel Noriega, Clifford Carr, Adriana Lamar
- *The Vampire's Ghost* (1945) John Abbott, Roy Barcroft, Peggy Stewart
- *Devil Bat's Daughter* (1946) Rosemary La Planche, John James, Michael Hale
- *Abbott and Costello Meet Frankenstein* (1948) Bud Abbott, Lou Costello, Lon Chaney Jr., Bela Lugosi

The 1950s: Drac Attack!

Coming off a decade of classically eccentric vamp flicks, the 1950s started out with a bang and just kept going. A large contingent of foreign films made their mark on the vampire legacy, and with them began a new renaissance of the vampire film as a cinematic stronghold. For example, the 1958 film *Blood of the Vampire* serves as an introduction to the striking Barbara Steele, who would later become one of horror's most recognizable scream queens and a consummate vampire witch in Mario Bava's 1960 cult classic *Black Sunday* (see Chapter 8).

While there were many classic Draculas to emerge from the 1950s, there is one that arguably stands fang and cape above the rest and can be summed up in two words: Christopher Lee. In 1958, Lee rose from the grave and made his vampiric debut in the Hammer film *Horror of Dracula* (also called *Dracula*).

Fresh off a stint playing the monster to Peter Cushing's Baron Victor Frankenstein in the 1957 *The Curse of Frankenstein*, Lee was again partnered with Cushing in *Horror*. The result was one of the best Dracula movies to date and the birth of what many assert is the most epic partnership in horror history (see Chapter 8). The film was also a turning point for Hammer, marking the beginnings of their dominance in the horror genre for over a decade.

Unlike Bela Lugosi's count in the 1931 version, Lee, with his graying locks, red eyes, and bloodthirsty hypnotics proved to be a stunning Dracula whose athleticism, seductiveness, and raw animal instincts brought new life to the character, while also proving to be an admirable foe to Cushing's equally provocative, action-oriented Van Helsing. Audiences were enamored by director Terence Fisher's interpretation, and the social subtext of the demise of the aristocracy of the nineteenth century. Films of the fabulous fifties are well worth watching, especially the following selections:

- *The Thing From Another World* (1951) Kenneth Tobey, Margaret Sheridan, James Arness
- *Old Mother Riley Meets the Vampire* (1952) Arthur Lucan, Bela Lugosi, Dora Bryan
- *Blood of Dracula* (1957) Sandra Harrison, Louise Lewis, Gail Ganley
- *Revenge of the Vampire*, aka *Dendam Pontianak* (1957, Singapore) Maria Menado, Puteh Lawak, S. M. Wahid
- *The Vampire*, aka *Mark of the Vampire* (1957) John Beal, Coleen Gray, Kenneth Tobey

- *The Vampire*, aka *Pontianak* (1957, Singapore) Maria Menado, M. Amin, Salmah Ahmad
- *Blood of the Vampire* (1958) Donald Wolfit, Vincent Ball, Barbara Shelley
- *Horror of Dracula*, aka *Dracula* (1958) Christopher Lee, Peter Cushing, Michael Gough, Melissa Stribling
- *The Vampire's Curse*, aka *Sumpah Pontianak* (1958) Maria Menado, Mustaffa Maarof, Salmah Ahmad
- *Hard Times for Dracula*, aka *Uncle Was a Vampire*, aka *Tempi duri per i vampiri* (1959, Italian satire) Christopher Lee, Renato Rascel, Sylva Koscina

The 1960s: Revival of the Fittest

The success of Christopher Lee's portrayal of Dracula breathed new life into the vampire genre, and for the next two decades, vamps, scamps, and various ghoulish creatures would grace the silver screen with style, humor, and plenty of creative license. The silver screen vampire continued its onslaught throughout the sixties, with a variety of filmmakers from around the world staking claim to the Dracula legend.

In 1960, Peter Cushing reprised his role of Abraham Van Helsing in the classic Hammer film *The Brides of Dracula*, only this time, the immortal fiend took on a different look, which to this day is debated as to whether or not it proved effective. David Peel's appearance as the wicked Baron Meinster stands in direct contrast to Lee's tall, dark, and deadly Dracula.

Peel was blonde, blue-eyed, and to the viewing audience, decidedly *not* Christopher Lee. *Brides* remains a cult favorite, however, if for no other reason than Cushing continues his legacy as Van Helsing with the class and active instinctiveness of a true vampire hunter (see Chapter 8).

> Lee, who spent his time becoming the leading horror star of his era, returned to his Transylvanian roots in 1966, again teaming up with director Terence Fisher for *Dracula: Prince of Darkness*, and also appeared in a handful of additional films including *The Castle of the Living Dead*, *Dr. Terror's House of Horrors*, *Theatre of Death*, *The Blood Demon*, and *Dracula Has Risen From the Grave*.

In 1964, legendary horror master Vincent Price starred in *The Last Man on Earth*, a film based on Richard Matheson's novel *I Am Legend*. Matheson himself was a cowriter of the script for the 1964 outing. Fighting against vampire zombies, Price's turn as Robert Neville would be reprised in 1971 by Charleton Heston in *The Omega Man*, and again by Will Smith in the 2007 blockbuster *I Am Legend*.

For a true dose of classic Swinging Sixties vampirism be sure to check out the following:

- *Black Sunday*, aka *La Maschera del demonio*, aka *Mask of the Demon* (1960, Italy) Barbara Steele, John Richardson, Ivo Garrani
- *The Brides of Dracula* (1960) Peter Cushing, Yvonne Monlaur, David Peel
- *The Vampire Returns*, aka *Pontianak Kembali* (1963, Singapore) Maria Menado, Malik Selamat
- *Castle of Blood*, aka *Danza macabra* (1964, Italy) Barbara Steele, Georges Rivière, Margarete Robsahm
- *The Castle of the Living Dead*, aka *Il Castello dei morti vivi* (1964, Italy) Christopher Lee, Gaia Germani, Philippe Leroy
- *The Last Man on Earth* (1964) Vincent Price, Franca Bettoia, Emma Danieli
- *Terror in the Crypt* (1964) Adriana Ambesi, Christopher Lee, Ursula Davis
- *Dr. Terror's House of Horrors* (1965) Peter Cushing, Christopher Lee, Donald Sutherland
- *Billy the Kid versus Dracula* (1966) John Carradine, Chuck Courtney, Melinda Plowman

- *Dracula: Prince of Darkness* (1966) Christopher Lee, Barbara Shelley, Andrew Keir
- *Theatre of Death*, aka *Blood Fiend* (1966) Christopher Lee, Julian Glover, Lelia Goldoni
- *Dr. Terror's Gallery of Horrors* (1967) Lon Chaney Jr., John Carradine
- *The Fearless Vampire Killers*, aka *Pardon Me, But Your Teeth Are in My Neck* (1967) Jack McGowran, Roman Polanski, Sharon Tate
- *The Blood Beast Terror* (1968) Peter Cushing, Robert Flemying, Wanda Ventham
- *Carmilla* (1968, Sweden) Monica Nordquist, Birger Malmsten
- *Dracula Has Risen from the Grave* (1968) Christopher Lee, Rupert Davies, Veronica Carlson
- *Blood of Dracula's Castle* (1969) Alexander D'Arcy, John Carradine, Paula Raymond

Cute, Campy, and Cunning

No doubt you're somewhat amazed by the long history that vampires have had at the movies. Indeed there are hundreds more films in addition to those that are highlighted. From its inception during the Silent Era through the Swinging Sixties, the cinematic vampire has benefited by its distinct evolution as a prime time protagonist. In the next chapter, you'll see how that evolution continues. From the 1970s to the present day, a Pandora's box of vampires and vampirism is opened—and there's no closing the lid. They're cute, they're spooky, and they're just waiting to hypnotize you!

Chapter 10

Reel-Time: The Seventies Through the New Millennium

As you've learned in the previous chapters, early vampires left a lasting impression on the world of cinema. Now it's time for you to enter the world of the modern-day vampires, where from the 1970s to the present day, an amazing preternatural explosion of vamps sucked their way through everything from horror to comedy. What you might be most impressed by is how truly immortal the vampire has become, serving up a strong dose of romance, *Matrix*-like action, black comedy, teen screamers, and even a cheerleader named Buffy to lead them on.

Modern-Day Immortals

The vampire genre of films is indeed immortal in regard to movie-making history, having begun with the Silent Era in 1896. From the 1930s through the 1960s, the genre grew stronger, in part as a result of both international and domestic filmmakers casting a wide net over Bram Stoker's historical character and also with the emergence of Hammer Films— which you learned about in Chapter 7—and their churning out one horror flick after another.

Beginning in the seventies, despite the fact that Hammer productions began to slide, that trend continued and moved on throughout the following decades in a natural progression that would see vampires and vampirism brought to new levels of intrigue, action, comedy, and otherworldly proportions.

The 1970s: Groovy, Gory, and Ghoulishly Grand!

If you've ever watched reruns of *The Brady Bunch* or *The Love Boat*, then you know all about how wacky and tacky seventies programming could get. The vampire genre is no exception, with its enormous mixed bag of vamp flicks jam-packed with everything from traditional Draculas to a post-apocalyptic blood scourge to epic battles between Frankenstein and the Wolf Man to campy vamps, kung fu vampirism, a vampire musical, and even a *Dracula* adaptation geared toward the hearing impaired. The wide variety of films speaks to the fact that so many vampire flicks were being made that filmmakers were in danger of beating immortal bad boys into an early grave. (At least until they could be resurrected!)

For starters, the 1970s introduced us to another of the Hammer Films' brood—the ineffable Polish actress Ingrid Pitt, who first appeared in the 1970 film *The Vampire Lovers* and again in 1971 in one of the four tales comprising *The House That Dripped Blood*. That same year, Pitt took yet another bite out of the genre, playing the lead in *Countess Dracula* (see Chapter 8). In 1972, the first substantial African American bloodsucker bared his fangs in *Blacula* and again a year later in the sequel *Scream Blacula Scream*. In both installments, Blacula was played by William Marshall with a cast of African American actors who used the films as a springboard to bigger future endeavors (see Chapter 5).

Also part of the prestigious mix of actors lending their talents to the world of the undead are Jonathan Frid as Barnabas Collins (in the 1970 *House of Dark Shadows* and 1971 *Night of Dark Shadows*), Robert Quarry (as *Count Yorga, Vampire* in 1970 and in *The Return of Count Yorga* the following year), Jack Palance (in the 1973 television premiere of *Bram Stoker's Dracula*), Udo Kier (in the bizarre 1974 outing *Andy Warhol's Dracula*), David Niven (as the hysterical "Old Dracula" in the 1974 film *Vampira*), and Louis Jourdan (in *Count Dracula* as part of Great Performances in 1977).

Worthy of special note in this explosion of bloodthirsty ghouls are two actors who are often singled out for their 1979 performances. The first is George Hamilton for his over-the-top Count in *Love at First Bite*, the tenth highest grossing vampire film of all-time (see Chapter 8). The second is that of Frank Langella in *Dracula*, which ranks at number eighteen on the all-time list. This film is widely considered to be one of the best in the vampire genre, with Langella giving a smoldering portrayal in a remake of Lugosi's 1931 *Dracula* which played off the Hamilton Deane and John Balderston theatrical productions (see Chapters 7 and 8).

Yet another cult favorite graced the big screen in this decade, offering up a new take on the vampire hunter and setting a standard for those who would follow. The 1974 film *Captain Kronos: Vampire Hunter* features dashing German actor Horst Janson as the suave and debonair Kronos, and John Cater as his hunchbacked sidekick Professor Grost. What makes this outing so fun and memorable is director Brian Clemens's melding of several film genres, most notably a type of Western with hints of traditional mystery, romance, science fiction, and Count of Monte Cristo swordplay all interwoven amid a steady dose of drama and cliché. For true vampire aficionados, *Captain Kronos* is a must-see.

It's not often that filmmakers can break entirely new barriers in the mainstream industry, but the 1975 film *Deafula* did just that. *Deafula* is the brainchild of its director, writer, and star Peter Wolf Wechsberg (cited under the name Peter Wolf), who is himself deaf. Unchallenged in its unique approach to filmmaking, *Deafula* is the first-ever feature film conveyed entirely in sign language.

So if you're up for a few good shivers, scores of naughty nightcrawlers, and some big laughs, you don't want to miss a few of the vampy, campy, artistic, and fantastic films of the seventies, including:

- *Count Yorga, Vampire* (1970) Robert Quarry, Roger Perry, Michael Murphy
- *Countess Dracula* (1970) Ingrid Pitt, Nigel Green, Sandor Elès
- *House of Dark Shadows* (1970) Jonathan Frid, Grayson Hall, Kathryn Leigh Scott
- *Scars of Dracula* (1970) Christopher Lee, Dennis Waterman, Jenny Hanley
- *Taste the Blood of Dracula* (1970) Christopher Lee, Geoffrey Keen, Gwen Watford
- *The Vampire Lovers* (1970) Ingrid Pitt, George Cole, Peter Cushing, Kate O'Mara
- *Dracula vs. Frankenstein* (1971) J. Carrol Naish, Lon Chaney Jr., Zandor Vorkov
- *The House That Dripped Blood* (England 1971) Christopher Lee, Peter Cushing, Denholm Elliott, John Bennett
- *Lust for a Vampire* (1971) Ralph Bates, Barbara Jefford, Suzanna Leigh
- *Night of Dark Shadows* (1971) Jonathan Frid, Grayson Hall, David Selby
- *The Omega Man* (1971) Charleton Heston, Anthony Zerbe, Rosalind Cash

- *The Return of Count Yorga* (1971) Robert Quarry, Mariette Hartley, Roger Perry
- *Twins of Evil* (1971) Peter Cushing, Damien Thomas, Madeleine and Mary Collinson
- *Blacula* (1972) William Marshall, Vonetta McGee, Denise Nicholas
- *Dracula A.D. 1972* (1972) Christopher Lee, Peter Cushing, Stephanie Beacham, Christopher Neame
- *The Night Stalker* (1972) Darren McGavin, Simon Oakland, Carol Lynley
- *Bram Stoker's Dracula* (1973) Jack Palance, Simon Ward, Nigel Davenport
- *Lemora: A Child's Tale of the Supernatural* (1973) Lesley Gilb, Cheryl Smith, William Whitton
- *The Satanic Rites of Dracula* (1973) Christopher Lee, Peter Cushing, Michael Coles, Joanna Lumley
- *Scream, Blacula, Scream* (1973) William Marshall, Don Mitchell, Pam Grier
- *Blood for Dracula*, aka *Andy Warhol's Dracula* (1974) Joe Dallesandro, Udo Kier, Arno Juerging
- *Captain Kronos: Vampire Hunter* (1974) Horst Janson, John Carson, Shane Briant
- *The Legend of the Seven Golden Vampires* (1974, kung fu vampirism!) Peter Cushing, David Chiang, Julie Ege
- *Son of Dracula*, aka *Count Downe*, aka *Son of Dracula* (1974 musical) Harry Nilsson, Ringo Starr, Dennis Price, Peter Frampton, Keith Moon
- *Vampira*, aka *Old Dracula* (1974) David Niven, Teresa Graves, Peter Bayliss
- *Deafula* (1975) Peter Wolf, Gary R. Holstrom, Lee Darel
- *Count Dracula* (1977) Louis Jourdan, Frank Finlay, Susan Penhaligon
- *Dracula* (1979) Frank Langella, Laurence Olivier, Donald Pleasence, Kate Nelligan
- *Love at First Bite* (1979) George Hamilton, Susan Saint James, Richard Benjamin
- *Salem's Lot* (1979) David Soul, James Mason, Lance Kerwin

The 1980s: Campy, Vampy, and Trampy

No doubt you'll recognize the infamous names Michael Myers, Freddy Krueger, and Jason Vorhees, who began their long-standing cinematic onslaught during the 1980s. But despite the overwhelming presence of that infamous horror trio, a few vampires managed to make their presence known.

Lacking the classic charm of their predecessors of the fifties, sixties, and seventies, eighties bloodsuckers, like so many disco songs, are often left to obscurity. But as with all film genres of the time, there are a few gems hidden in the shadows, several of which are cult classics.

One of these is the 1983 film *The Hunger*, an artistic and overly sumptuous tale based on Whitley Strieber's 1981 novel of the same name. It stars the timeless Catherine Deneuve, arguably one of the best female vampires of all time, as Miriam Blaylock, a cold-blooded alien vampire of ancient Egyptian origin now residing in New York (see Chapters 6 and 8).

In 1985, came the fun and campy horrorfest known as *Fright Night*, featuring Roddy McDowall as a former horror star, William Ragsdale as a teenage horror fan, and Susan Sarandon's former husband, Chris Sarandon, as the "real" vampire they must conquer. *Fright Night* was a commercial success, raking in close to $25 million and ranking sixteenth on the all-time vampire movie list. Its 1989 sequel didn't fare quite as well but remains in the top fifty.

Of the vamp films of the eighties, a handful still maintain rankings on the all-time list, including Jim Carrey's 1985 comedy *Once Bitten*, the Jeff Goldblum vampire spoof *Transylvania 6-5000* also in 1985, and the frightening brood of Southern bloodsuckers featured in Kathryn Bigelow's 1987 offering *Near Dark*. What did prove to be a box office success in 1987 was director Joel Schumacher's *The Lost Boys*, a vamp flick with decidedly more comedy than drama that pits teen vampires against teen vampire hunters in a small coastal community dubbed the "murder capital of the world." A cult fave to be certain, the film grossed over $32 million.

Here are a few vampy flicks of the eighties you might get a chuckle out of:

- *The Hunger* (1983) Catherine Deneuve, David Bowie, Susan Sarandon
- *Fright Night* (1985) Roddy McDowall, Chris Sarandon, William Ragsdale
- *Lifeforce* (1985) Steve Railsback, Peter Firth, Mathilda May
- *Once Bitten* (1985) Lauren Hutton, Jim Carrey, Cleavon Little
- *Transylvania 6-5000* (1985) Jeff Goldblum, Geena Davis, Joseph Bologna, Carol Kane
- *Vampire Hunter D*, aka *Banpaia hanta* (1985, Japanese anime) Kaneto Shiozawa, Michael McConnohie
- *The Lost Boys* (1987) Jason Patric, Corey Haim, Kiefer Sutherland, Dianne Weist
- *Near Dark* (1987) Adrian Pasdar, Lance Henriksen, Bill Paxton
- *A Return to Salem's Lot* (1987) Michael Moriarty, Ricky Addison Reed, Samuel Fuller
- *Fright Night Part 2* (1988) Roddy McDowall, William Ragsdale, Julie Carmen
- *My Best Friend Is a Vampire* (1988) Robert Sean Leonard, Rene Auberjonois, Cheryl Pollack
- *Vampire's Kiss* (1989) Nicolas Cage, Maria Conchita Alonso, Jennifer Beals.

The 1990s: Buffy, Blade, and Big-Time Bad Boys!

As you can see, the eighties gave us a chaotic mix of vampire movies, which meant that the nineties were primed and ready for a resurgence of movies that would bring the world of the undead back to its roots.

If there's one nineties vamp flick that fits the bill, it's Francis Ford Coppola's 1992 *Bram Stoker's Dracula*, a stylish and taut retelling of Stoker's masterpiece with an exceptional cast and stellar performance by Gary Oldman, who as Prince Vlad is one of the best bloodsuckers ever to the grace the silver screen (see Chapter 8).

In this telling, *Dracula* begins in 1462 in Transylvania with Vlad the Impaler's tragedy and transformation before moving to the late 1800s to imprison Jonathan Harker (Keanu Reeves) and Vlad's embarkation to London to pursue Harker's fiancée Mina (Winona Ryder), the reincarnation of Vlad's beloved wife Elisabeta. Along the way, Vlad must deal with the traditional Stoker characters and match wits with Abraham Van Helsing, a role that would've suited no other actor than the brilliant Anthony Hopkins.

Tom Waits's performance as Renfield is perhaps one of the most underrated of the historic cinematic Renfields. With its stunning visual appeal, tense story line and action sequences, and strong seductive undercurrent, this *Dracula* rendition is a must for all vampire aficionados.

Two years later, in 1994, yet another blockbuster arrived in the long-awaited film adaptation of Anne Rice's best-selling novel *Interview with the Vampire: The Vampire Chronicles*. Much ado was publicly made by Rice herself when the final casting was announced, but she later recanted her comments after viewing the film.

Did you know that the casting of *Interview* had been bantered about for over thirty years? During the late seventies it was John Travolta who was said to have been slated as the film's star. Rice herself over the years made mention of Rutger Hauer, Jeremy Irons, and Daniel Day-Lewis taking part. It's also said that for the big-screen version, Johnny Depp was offered the part!

Whether you agree with the casting of Tom Cruise and Brad Pitt or not, it must be said that what resulted was a lush if not accurate portrayal of Lestat, who aside from Stoker's

Dracula, is the best-known vampire in this and other worlds (see Chapters 6 and 8).

Coming in third on the all-time box office vampire gross with a take of over $105 million as compared to Coppola's fourth place ranking at over $82 million, *Interview* is faithful to the novel, and rife with the interplay of Lestat's arrogance matched up against Louis's pensiveness and the wickedness of their daughter Claudia, played by Kirsten Dunst.

The nineties also gave us our first glimpse of the popular franchise that would become *Buffy the Vampire Slayer*. A feature film in 1992, it stars Kristy Swanson, Donald Sutherland, and Rutger Hauer. One of the top twenty all-time grossing vamp flicks, *Buffy* launched the popular television franchise and Buffy's star Sarah Michelle Gellar (see Chapters 6 and 11).

The year 1998 marks the arrival of one of the more innovative and popular vampire-human hybrids, who kicks some serious bloodsucker booty. As with most vampires, he's known by a single name—Blade—and he's a force to be reckoned with (see Chapter 8). Starring Wesley Snipes, *Blade* is adapted from the character who first appeared in Marvel Comics in July of 1973 in *Tomb of Dracula*.

In *Blade*, his fight against an evil underground network of hard-core vampires casts him as a necessary but somewhat reluctant hero that carries through both sequels, *Blade II* in 2002 and *Blade: Trinity* in 2004.

We now introduce you to a few of the more renowned vamp flicks of the nineties:

- *Nightlife* (1990) Ben Cross, Maryam D'Abo, Keith Szarabajka
- *My Grandfather Is a Vampire* (1991, New Zealand) Al Lewis, Justin Gocke, Milan Borich
- *Subspecies* (1991) Anders Hove, Angus Scrimm, Laura Mae Tate
- *Bram Stoker's Dracula* (1992) Gary Oldman, Anthony Hopkins, Winona Ryder

- *Buffy the Vampire Slayer* (1992) Kristy Swanson, Donald Sutherland, Rutger Hauer
- *Innocent Blood* (1992) Anne Parillaud, Chazz Palminteri, Anthony LaPaglia, Robert Loggia
- *Bloodstone: Subspecies II* (1993) Anders Hove, Denice Duff, Kevin Blair
- *Bloodlust: Subspecies III* (1994) Anders Hove, Denice Duff, Kevin Blair
- *Interview with the Vampire: The Vampire Chronicles* (1994) Tom Cruise, Brad Pitt, Kirsten Dunst
- *Dracula: Dead and Loving It* (1995) Leslie Nielsen, Peter MacNicol, Harvey Korman, Amy Yasbeck
- *Vampire in Brooklyn* (1995) Eddie Murphy, Angela Bassett, Allen Payne
- *From Dusk Till Dawn* (1996) Harvey Keitel, George Clooney, Quentin Tarantino
- *Blade* (1998) Wesley Snipes, Stephen Dorff, Kris Kristofferson
- *John Carpenter's Vampires* (1998) James Woods, Daniel Baldwin, Sheryl Lee
- *Subspecies 4: Bloodstorm* (1998) Anders Hove, Denice Duff, Jonathon Morris
- *From Dusk Till Dawn 2: Texas Blood Money* (1999) Robert Patrick, Bo Hopkins, Duane Whitaker
- *From Dusk Till Dawn 3: The Hangman's Daughter* (1999) Marco Leonardi, Michael Parks, Temuera Morrison

The New Millennium: Hip and Horrifically Romantic

The turn of the century featured a new strain of vampire cinema, and while many films and filmmakers paid homage to their distinguished predecessors by retaining some portion of the Dracula legend, many surprised us with innovative twists, bigger and better monsters courtesy of innovative CGI techniques, slick Japanese anime, and a few kick-butt female action heroes.

In 2000, we were treated to *Shadow of the Vampire*, a film that paid its respects to the 1922 silent film classic, *Nosferatu* (see Chapter 7). In *Shadow*, Willem Dafoe takes on the role of Max Schreck, the actor who played Count Orlock in *Nosferatu*, and the purported real-life turmoil that came with his relationship to *Nosferatu's* director F.W. Murnau (played by the appropriately creepy John Malkovich) during the silent film's production. So compelling was Dafoe's performance that he garnered an Oscar nomination for Best Actor. Hardly the standard for a vampire flick.

Though it was panned by critics when it hit the big screen in 2004, *Van Helsing* proved to be no slouch at the box office, garnering over $120 million and becoming the second highest grossing vampire film of all time. Taking very little from the Van Helsing legacy of Peter Cushing or Edward Van Sloan, Aussie heartthrob Hugh Jackman transformed himself into an action superhero of supernatural proportions. For pure fun and a visual CGI feast, you don't want to miss the action-packed romp that is *Van Helsing*.

A fast and furious horrorfest, the film finds Van Helsing in the secret employ of the Vatican during the late 1800s, as a somewhat conflicted hired gun of the underworld. As such, Gabriel Van Helsing has the unenviable job of hunting down the crème de la crème of paranormal perpetrators, including a rather bulked-up Mr. Hyde, a sympathetic Frankenstein, and of course, Dracula.

In what would prove to be an epic battle of werewolf versus vampire, and with the help of Anna Valerious, a gypsy princess played by Kate Beckinsale, Van Helsing ventures to Transylvania to take on Count Vladislaus Dracula, played to the hilt by Richard Roxburgh (see Chapter 8).

What makes Jackman's interpretation of Van Helsing intriguing is the plot twist, whereby Dracula, through his taunting, helps Van Helsing regain his lost memories of how he came to be—a revelation with, shall we say, eternally angelic consequences. Despite its lack of critical acclaim, *Van Helsing* proves yet again that Bram Stoker's legendary conception continues to provide inspiration while also keeping vampire fans firmly seated at the edge of their coffins. And besides that—Hugh Jackman *is* the ultimate action-horror hottie!

In the 2000s, we were also introduced to a new kind of vampiric chick in Kate Beckinsale, who transforms herself into Selene, the rebellious "death dealer" and star of 2003's *Underworld* and its 2006 sequel, *Underworld: Evolution*, both of which are ranked ninth and seventh respectively on the all-time top-grossing vamp flicks and thrust Beckinsale into the vampire Hall of Fame (see Chapter 8).

Along those same lines, only with a distinctly futuristic sci-fi bent is Milla Jovovich's turn in the 2006 tour de force, *Ultraviolet*. In the film, Violet stands alone amid a raging war between a totalitarian late twenty-first century government and a sub-faction of individuals at the bad end of biological warfare experimentation that resulted in a vampire-like disease.

With its graphic novel style, primary colors, and *Matrix/Aeon Flux*-type aura, *Ultraviolet* is hands-down one of the most succulent and mind-blowing films to date. As one of the infected "Hemophages," Violet's sole purpose is protecting a young boy and seeking revenge for her kind. Vampire fans should hunt down the uncut version of *Ultraviolet*, which more fully draws on the vampiric aspect of the plot.

Yet another crossover of the vampiric horror and sci-fi genre is the third remake of Richard Matheson's 1954 novel *I Am Legend*. For Matheson's concept, the third time was the charm. Will Smith's 2007 portrayal as military virologist Robert Neville in *I Am Legend* was a blockbuster, amassing over $256 million at the box office and making it the highest-grossing vampire film in history.

As for the present day, everyone is eagerly anticipating the 2008 winter release of the screen adaptation of Stephenie Meyer's novel *Twilight*, a modern-day twist on *Romeo and Juliet*, featuring Bella, a young high school girl in love with Edward, a stunning young lad who, as luck would have it, happens to be a vampire (see Chapter 6).

Let's take a look at some of the bloodsucking cinema the new millennium has offered up thus far:

- *Dracula 2000* (2000) Gerard Butler, Christopher Plummer, Jonny Lee Miller, Justine Waddell
- *Shadow of the Vampire* (2000) Willem Dafoe, John Malkovich, Udo Kier, Cary Elwes
- *Vampire Hunter D: Bloodlust* (2000, Japanese anime) Hideyuki Tanaka, Ichirô Nagai, Kôichi Yamadera
- *The Forsaken* (2001) Kerr Smith, Brendan Fehr, Izabella Miko
- *Hellsing,* aka *Herushingu* (2001, Japanese anime) Jôji Nakata, Yoshiko Sakakibara, Fumiko Orikasa
- *Blade II* (2002) Wesley Snipes, Kris Kristofferson, Leonor Varela
- *Queen of the Damned* (2002) Stuart Townsend, Lena Olin, Marguerite Moreau, Vincent Perez
- *Underworld* (2003) Kate Beckinsale, Scott Speedman, Michael Sheen, Bill Nighy
- *Blade: Trinity* (2004) Wesley Snipes, Kris Kristofferson, Dominic Purcell, Jessica Biel
- *Van Helsing (*2004) Hugh Jackman, Kate Beckinsale, Richard Roxburgh
- *BloodRayne* (2005) Kristanna Loken, Michael Madsen, Matt Davis, Udo Kier
- *Hellsing Ultimate OVA Series* (2006, Japanese anime series) Jôji Nakata, Yoshiko Sakakibara, Fumiko Orikasa
- *Ultraviolet* (2006) Milla Jovovich, Cameron Bright, Nick Chinlund
- *Underworld: Evolution* (2006) Kate Beckinsale, Scott Speedman, Tony Curran
- *BloodRayne II: Deliverance* (2007) Natassia Malthe, Zack Ward, Michael Paré
- *I Am Legend* (2007) Will Smith, Alice Braga, Abby (Sam the dog)
- *30 Days of Night* (2007) Josh Hartnett, Melissa George, Danny Huston
- *The Lost Boys: The Tribe* (2008) Tad Hilgenbrink, Angus Sutherland, Autumn Reeser
- *Twilight* (2008) Kristen Stewart, Robert Pattinson, Taylor Lautner

SMALL-SCREEN SCREAMERS

So in your wildest dreams, did you ever guess that vampires have been flying across the silver screen for over a hundred years? For a creature evolved from lore and fiction, that's a bitingly big accomplishment. More than likely, you've spent plenty of time mesmerized by many of the children of the night. Now that you've had a peek into the big screen crypt of the vampire, it's time to sink your chompers into the realm of the television vampire, from made-for-TV movies and mini-series to kiddie nosferatu and some of the most beloved television series in history.

Chapter 11

Small-Screen Bloodsuckers

Given the sheer volume of silver screen vampires, it was only a matter of time before they sharpened their fangs and donned their cloaks strictly for television audiences. As a result, scores of bloodsucking bad boys and bombshells clawed their way out of their crypts and into our homes. And while made-for-television vamps have always been around, it wasn't until the last two decades that they've begun to gain an immortal following. Ready or not, here are a host of television vamps who've taken a big bite out of prime-time programming.

Early Television Vampires

Because of the success silver screen nightcrawlers have had, it's easy to see why, with the onset of television, vampires gained even more exposure as those classic films finally made it into our collective living rooms. As more and more of us became exposed to vampires, so too did television programmers, who staked a claim in several vampiric characters and series that served to set the stage for public acceptance of the vampire taking part in everything from cartoons to made-for-TV movies to weekly serials and even a legendary gothic soap opera. It was indeed that soap opera that got the public's hemoglobin churning and gave television watchers their first shadowed glimpse of how truly mesmerizing a television vamp could be. But audiences got their first official taste of television bloodsuckers in the form of comedy, and a wacky family known simply as *The Munsters*.

The Munsters

The year 1964 marks the arrival of two of the most unique and legendary families to ever appear on the small screen—the eccentric and macabre Addams Family and the lovable, wacky bunch known as the Munsters. Paying homage to the horror genre by spoofing some of its most delicious characters and concepts, both families gave audiences two years of solid laughs and a new appreciation for the humor of what most individuals conceive of as horrifying.

Without a doubt, *The Munsters* provided a brilliant way of easing the public into accepting vampires as leading characters. Fred Gwynne, Yvonne De Carlo, Al Lewis, Butch Patrick, and Pat Priest were transformed into a Frankenstein-type monster, father-daughter vampires, a werewolf, and a perfectly human niece.

Housed together in their spooky abode at 1313 Mockingbird Lane, the Munsters had everything a monster could hope for: a Grandpa who hung from the rafters like a bat, a pet bat named Igor, a dragon named Spot, and even a car nicknamed "Drag-u-la," likely an homage to Grandpa's last name and Lily's maiden name—Dracula. Even legendary Dracula portrayer John Carradine made a few guest appearances as one of Herman's bosses at the funeral parlor where he was employed.

Even funnier was the opening segment to the show, which featured Lily parodying the opener to the Donna Reed show, making light of the notion that the Munsters were just like any other red-blooded American family. Though the series, like *The Addams Family*, only lasted two seasons, both left an indelible mark on television history with reruns still playing daily.

> Even more spectacular is the fact that Herman Munster was ranked nineteenth in *TV Guide*'s June 2004 issue of "The 50 Greatest TV Dads of All Time." Pretty impressive for a big, clumsy, green-colored goofball!

DARK SHADOWS

If you're a big soap opera fan, then you must check out one of the most innovative soaps in history. In 1966, audiences were treated to a new kind of vampire, a more dark and dramatic breed whose sinister past eventually turns him into the characteristic reluctant vampire. That bloodsucker is Barnabas Collins and he is the star of the gothic television soap opera *Dark Shadows*.

Now, it's no mystery that soap operas have unbelievably huge followings, with fans hanging on every actor's word, action, interview, and convention appearance. *Dark Shadows* almost missed that fanfare, when after six months it was faced with cancellation. It was at that point that the supernatural element was introduced, with Barnabas's arrival at Collinwood.

Running every weekday afternoon on ABC from June of 1966 through April of 1971, *Dark Shadows* became a cult classic that to this day retains its immortality through major Internet fan sites, fan clubs, societies, conventions, CD audio dramas, DVDs, reruns, and a pair of feature-length films: *House of Dark Shadows* in 1970 and *Night of Dark Shadows* in 1971. The series also spawned a short-lived television remake in 1991, comic books, and a slew of serialized novels.

What's truly unique about *Dark Shadows*, among many aspects, is its telenovela style and live-to-tape format with complex overlapping character arcs, time travel, séances, a parallel universe, ghosts, witches, werewolves, and dream and fantasy sequences that took the story from present-day Collinsport, Maine, to its late 1700s colonial roots and beyond.

Throughout all of the plotlines spread among over 1,200 episodes, the repertoire of actors involved playing multiple roles—typically their own ancestors—squeezing out every ounce of melodrama they could muster. So groundbreaking was the series, that even Robert Cobert's eerie soundtrack ranked on *Billboard's* Top 20 charts in 1969, with one of the tracks earning Cobert a Grammy nomination.

THE COLLINWOOD PHENOMENA

The series begins when governess Victoria Winters arrives at Collinwood estate to care for a young boy named David Collins. Surrounded by a rather eccentric and secretive family, strange occurrences begin almost immediately, setting the stage for all the dark drama to follow.

After six months and sagging ratings, *Dark Shadows* creator Dan Curtis took the bold step of introducing a 200-year-old vampire into the mix, which though radical at the time, turned the entire series rightside up. Actor Jonathan Frid—who has built an entire career off his fiend—made his first appearance in episode 211 as Barnabas Collins, a vampire released from his slumber who arises to wreak havoc upon a new generation (see Chapter 8).

A tortured soul, Barnabas reintegrates himself into the wealthy Collins family by claiming to be a long-lost relative, and from there his story takes more twists and turns than a Swiss mountain road.

Cursed by the evil witch Angelique in the late 1700s, Barnabas bears many of the traditional trappings of the drawing-room bloodsucker, namely sleeping in a coffin, casting no reflection in mirrors, and the ability to transform into a bat. Naturally, the public became enamored with Barnabas and all the melodramatic characters and situations one would expect of a daytime soap. What may seem campy now was actually for its time a clever use of sets, costuming, makeup, and special effects that for a tape-and-go serial drama made up for the occasional appearance of a cameraman or microphone interrupting a scene.

DARK SHADOWS REDUX

Dark Shadows was canceled in 1971, but its cult following relentlessly clamored for more. The show was partially syndicated in 1975 and aired in syndication through 1990. For the next three years, all of the episodes were released to and aired by the Sci Fi Channel.

In 1991, twenty years after its cancellation, NBC ran a short-lived remake of the series in prime time. Again directed by Dan Curtis, and starring Ben Cross as Barnabas, Jean Simmons, Lysette Anthony, and 1960s scream queen Barbara Steele (see Chapter 8), the revival was a weekly series with a big budget.

Timing in this case proved its undoing, as Gulf War coverage caused the show's pre-empting and odd scheduling contributing to its inevitable demise after only a dozen episodes. The fact that the series ended with a whopper of a cliffhanger, of course, resulted in viewer outrage.

> With any luck, their exhortations will be answered by actor Johnny Depp, who so loved *Dark Shadows* as a child that he claimed he wanted to be Barnabas Collins. Depp's wish may come to fruition, as he recently announced he would play Jonathan Frid's legendary role in a *Dark Shadows* feature-length film which Depp's production company purchased the rights to in July 2008.

MADE-FOR-TELEVISION VAMPS

Over the decades, there have been dozens of made-for-television vampire movies that crossed all genres ranging from the 1996 comedy *Munster, Go Home!* to *Mom's Got a Date With a Vampire* (2000). The truth is, as you may have noticed, that never a week goes by without some type of vamp flick appearing on the tube. How good they are when measured against the classics is a subject that's always up for debate. As with all genres, however, there are always a few gems hidden in a mountain of cubic zirconia.

THE NIGHT STALKER

In the television vampire realm, that first gem was an unlikely 1972 television movie that spun off into a wildly popular late-night television series. The movie was *The Night Stalker*, and it starred legendary actor Darren McGavin as Carl Kolchak, the intrepid, bumbling, and relentlessly persistent reporter who attracts evil supernatural critters like a *vryokolakas* to a rotting corpse (see Chapter 1).

With a teleplay written by *I Am Legend* author Richard Matheson based on a novel by Jeff Rice, and directed by *Dark Shadows* creator Dan Curtis, the aptly titled *The Night Stalker* (no doubt referring to both the protagonist and antagonist) was enormously successful for ABC. In the film, Kolchak finds himself up against ancient Romanian vampire Janos Skorzeny who's prowling Vegas and sucking dry a score of young women until Kolchak himself stakes him.

The following year, in 1973, McGavin, along with Curtis, Matheson, and Rice once again teamed up for another Kolchak foray, *The Night Strangler*. The year 1974 marked the premiere of the television series *Kolchak: The Night Stalker*, with its third episode, titled "The Vampire," paying homage to Kolchak's vampiric skills by featuring a prostitute-turned-bloodsucker running amok in Las Vegas.

In September 2005, a remake of *Night Stalker* briefly appeared featuring *Queen of the Damned* star Stuart Townsend, but it was sadly pulled after only six episodes. No doubt, Kolchak himself would've attested that *some* things are better left untold.

DRAC IS BACK!

Another shining gem in the television vampiric realm is Jack Palance, who in 1973 donned cape and fangs to play Dracula in a winning version of Bram Stoker's novel, pulled together by the same talent who gave us *The Night Stalker*, director Dan Curtis and author Richard Matheson. As the legendary bad boy, Palance is by many accounts one of the best to ever play the role, his smoky voice coupled with his overpowering physical presence allowing him a command and confidence that only a select few Dracula portrayers have been able to channel (see Chapter 8).

In 1977, another television vampire of note took to the small screen in the form of renowned French actor Louis Jourdan, who starred in *Count Dracula*, a version produced by the BBC for its Great Performances series. Closely following Bram Stoker's legendary novel—more so than most adaptations—Jourdan brought many of the same subtleties to his Count as Frank Langella did to his 1979 portrayal (see Chapter 8).

Also premiering in prime time in 1979 was the adaptation of Stephen King's vampire extravaganza *Salem's Lot*, which focuses on a writer who returns to his hometown to find that something's not quite right with the haunted house on the hill. Starring David Soul, James Mason, and Lance Kerwin, *Salem's Lot*, like many of King's horror adaptations, has become a cult favorite in the vampire realm (see Chapter 6).

In 1990, Ben Cross took yet another turn in his coffin, playing Vlad to Maryam D'Abo's vampiric Angelique in the dark comedy *Nightlife*. Written by *Saturday Night Live* Emmy-winning writer Anne Beatts, the amusing romp finds Angelique ditching Vlad and awakening in Mexico City after a 100-year nap only to find that vampires are merely considered "diseased individuals." Of course, falling in love with her doctor creates a love triangle that makes for a bloody good time!

PRIME TIME SUCKERS

Given the very nature of vampires, specifically their propensities of bloodlust, seduction, and murder, it's easy to see why creatures of the night have a tough time getting past television mucky-mucks and particularly television censors. In regard to long-term vampiric success, there's no arguing that *Dark Shadows* has thus far had the longest run.

A few other series attempted a rise from the grave with short-lived success, including *Dracula: The Series* (1990), *Kindred: The Embraced* (based on the role playing game *Vampire: The Embraced*), and more recently, a single season of the 2007 drama *Moonlight* featuring a vampire private investigator.

But along the way, there have been a few highly successful vampire-based series whose characters have television immortality that, for shows like *Forever Knight*, *Angel*, and *Buffy the Vampire Slayer*, resulted in serialized novels, comic books, companion books, hugely popular Internet fan sites, fan clubs, societies, and launched franchises complete with bobbleheads, action figures, magazines, video games, conventions, and all measure of paraphernalia (see Chapter 6).

FOREVER KNIGHT

In 1989, the CBS made-for-TV movie *Nick Knight* gave us our first glimpse of one of the more tortured reluctant vampires ever conceived. The film starred musician and former *General Hospital* heartthrob Rick Springfield as a four-centuries-old vampire working in Los Angeles as a detective solving a host of grisly murders involving victims being drained of blood.

In 1992, the pilot was remade into the late-night series *Forever Knight*, with the affable Welsh-Canadian actor Geraint Wynn Davies assuming the lead role of homicide detective Nicholas Knight. Primarily a Canadian production, the plot differs from the pilot on several accounts in that it was based in Toronto and Nicholas is now 800 years old, a fact that only adds to his extreme angst in attempting to make restitution for his evil past and ultimately rid himself of his vampirism.

He's helped in his quest by pathologist and close mortal confidant Natalie Lambert (Catherine Disher), who stands in contrast to Nick's vampiric confidant and former lover Janette (Deborah Duchene).

Complicating matters throughout *Forever Knight's* three-season run is Nick's maker, the intensely philosophical and wickedly sinister Lucien LaCroix, brilliantly played by Nigel Bennett. A 2,000-year-old former Roman army general made in Pompeii during the eruption of Mt. Vesuvius, Lacroix's obvious disdain for Nick's quest for absolution and humanity beautifully portrays the misuse of vampiric power and its alternate usefulness as a tool for creating a better society.

Like many traditional vampires, those in *Forever Knight* have superhuman strength, hypnotic powers, heightened senses, and the typical aversion to sunlight and staking. They also possess the capacity for flight, moving at great speeds, and tissue regeneration.

What has arguably endeared *Forever Knight* to the hearts of all vampire aficionados, aside from the various love-hate triangles and vampiric antagonists, is the constant interplay between Nick and LaCroix, whose toying with mortals leads him to moonlight as "The Nightcrawler," a late-night radio host, in which his broadcasts invariably shed light on Nick's all-consuming pathos and fight to control his bloodlust and rage. Indoctrinated into the undead by LaCroix in 1228, Nicholas de Brabant remains one of the more high-profile vampires ever to grace the small screen.

THREE CHEERS FOR BUFFY!

When it comes to Valley Girls turned vampire hunters there's only one name that springs to mind: Buffy. In 1992, writer Joss Whedon introduced us to the self-obsessed, flitty, shopaholic cheerleader Buffy Summers in the feature-length film *Buffy the Vampire Slayer*. Cute and campy, the film stars Kristy Swanson, Donald Sutherland, and Rutger Hauer as the evil Lothos. Though Buffy proved successful at the box office, it was decidedly a flop in Whedon's mind, as his intent was not to create a high school horror romp, but an extraordinary embodiment of staunch female character.

Five years later, in 1997, Whedon got his chance as executive producer of the series *Buffy the Vampire Slayer*, which premiered on the small WB Network. For seven seasons, the Emmy-winning series gave us an empowered Buffy (played by Sarah Michelle Gellar), who kicked all kinds of demonic and vampiric booty in her hometown of Sunnydale, California, and beyond, focusing primarily on the "Hellmouth," a demonic gateway below Sunnydale High. As its most basic metaphor, one can't help but be amused by the idea of high school being equated to hell.

Amid all the campy comedy, drama, paranormal terror, and martial arts wrapped around scores of vampires and other miscreants, Buffy came to know Angel, played by the ever-charming David Boreanaz, whose serious immortal bad boy attitude rears its ugly head when he and Buffy engage in a night of passion. Tragic and metaphorical in its subtext, this meeting of vampire and vampire slayer proved so successful that it launched a spinoff, simply titled *Angel*.

What's truly extraordinary about Buffy is how financially successful the franchise has become. The term *Buffyverse* is used today to encompass all things Buffy-related. The Buffy-verse is huge in its offerings of fan sites, clubs, all conceivable paraphernalia, and scores of serialized novels based on the beloved Valley Girl vampire hunter (see Chapter 6).

GETTING ANGELIC

Premiering in 1999 on the WB, *Angel* highlighted the triumphs and extremely tortured soul of the 200-year-old vampire Angel, who spends his first millennia killing with reckless abandon but who, courtesy of a band of revenge-minded gypsies, has his human soul restored to his vampiric body.

An exceptional twist on vampire lore, Angel is tormented by the knowledge of his former murderous ways and is driven to help others as a private investigator in a quest to alleviate his eternal angst and remorse. With *Buffy* creator Joss Whedon at the helm, David Boreanaz truly shined as a tortured creature whose somber reckonings, memories, and killings showed the dichotomy of a reluctant vampire and also a vampire unwilling to forfeit his immortality so that he can continue making restitution to humanity.

Running for five seasons, *Angel*, like *Buffy*, achieved television immortality. Upon its cancellation, and prompted by fan outrage, Angel's ambiguous farewell resulted in a 2007 comic book series called *Angel: After the Fall*.

TRUE BLOOD

Though it's only just begun, HBO has high hopes for its new vampire series, *True Blood*, based on the *Sookie Stackhouse* series written by author Charlaine Harris (see Chapter 6). With its September 2008 premiere, *True Blood* introduced the world to the inhabitants of Bon Temps, a fictional town in Louisiana that is home to eccentric, reluctantly telepathic waitress Sookie Stackhouse, played by Oscar-winner Anna Paquin, and the man she falls in love with, Bill Compton (played by Stephen Moyer), who just happens to be a 173-year-old vampire. Of course, the fact that Bill's 148 years older than Sookie matters little, considering vampires, courtesy of the invention of synthetic blood by Japanese scientists, have now become accepted among society. After the airing of the first two episodes, it was announced that *True Blood* would return for a second season.

Kiddie Nosferatu

While the majority of traditional literary and cinematic vampires are considered too frightening for small children, there have been a number of programs that have introduced vampiric characters through cartoons such as *Scooby Doo* and even on *Sesame Street*, where the lovable purple Muppet Count von Count has been teaching kiddies how to count since the early 1970s. Modeled somewhat after Bela Lugosi's Dracula, the Count sports a pair of fangs, a monocle, a nifty goatee, and the ever-present black cape. The Count's obsessive need to count—whether intentional or not—harkens back to a popular folkloric practice of using seeds to keep a vampire at bay (see Chapter 5).

COUNT DUCKULA

One of the more innovative twists on the Dracula legend is the animated British cartoon *Count Duckula*, a spinoff of the popular 1981 to 1992 cartoon *Danger Mouse*. A clear parody of Dracula reworked for the kiddies, Duckula is an obsessive stage-struck vegetarian vampire duck who resides, naturally, in Castle Duckula with his bumbling vulture manservant Igor, and equally inept hen nursemaid called Nanny.

How Duckula came to be a vegetarian is that during the ritual for his resurrection, Nanny provided Igor with ketchup instead of blood, thereby rendering the daffy vampire more inclined to consume vegan fare rather than red-blooded victims. In hot pursuit of Duckula during his fame-seeking escapades is German goose and vampire hunter Dr. Von Goosewing. From 1988 to 1993, sixty-five episodes of *Count Duckula* were created, as well as a Marvel Comics version of the wacky vampiric quacker.

THE GROOVIE GOOLIES

Only in the seventies would you find a show with the word *groovy* in the title, which in this case refers to a band of animated monsters who constitute the *Groovie Goolies*. Spun off the very popular *Archie Show* and then combined with *Sabrina, the Teenage Witch* before branching out on their own, the Goolies are a motley crew, who room together at Horrible Hall. They include Bella LaGhostly, Drac, Mummy, Hagatha, Franklin "Frankie" Frankenstein, Wolfgang "Wolfie" Wolfman, the two-headed Doctor Jeckyll and Hyde, and animated skeleton Boneapart, among others. Based primarily on classic Universal horror films, the show aired in 1971, with several other specials presented over the years. Of course, being a literal band of monsters, each of its sixteen episodes ends with an original *Groovie Goolies* rock song.

Fanged and Flamboyant

While literature and lore give us the ability to picture in our minds the most romantic and heinous vampires in fictional history, it's ultimately film and television that put a name to a face. In this instance . . . a fanged face. As you've likely learned in the last few chapters, the immortal bad boy runs the gamut of interpretation in physical, spiritual, and emotional realms. But the bottom line is that no matter how frightening these interpretations are—they aren't real.

Or are they?

With all that you've now gleaned about immortals, it's time to examine the ups and downs of being part of the undead. Would you really want to be a vampire? What are the limitations and benefits? How can you tell if your neighbor is a nosferatu? All this and more in the next chapter.

Chapter 12

SO YOU WANNA BE A VAMPIRE?

With a range of superhuman abilities and a lifestyle that has such unearthly appeal, the vampire cuts a dramatic figure that some—especially vampire aficionados—would love to emulate if only for a day. For us mere mortals, the lure of immortality is intoxicating, and is perhaps the best reason for wanting to become *le vampyre*. But would you really do it? In this chapter, you'll learn the ups and downs of what it would be like to be one, along with a handy list of things to look for, to help you identify one. We begin, however, with the perils of immortality.

The Flipside of Immortality

If you were given the option to live forever in exchange for becoming a bloodthirsty creature of the night, would you do it? Being posed that question in a stable state of mind evokes serious thought about the pros and cons of immortality. Yeah, you could roam the planet, decade after decade, century after century, watching humanity evolve right before your very acute preternatural eyes. You could travel the world, indulge in the arts, live a sumptuous lifestyle, wear all the designer clothes you want, and partake and likely abuse all the superhuman powers you've been granted. So where's the downside?

Let's face it. Like any addiction, one tends to hit rock bottom. Is there such a thing as too much of a good thing? You bet. No matter how old a vampire you'd become, you'd have to struggle with the inevitable loneliness that comes with being an immortal, coupled with the reality that you must live with the fact that you're using the human race—the same race you were once part of—as your own personal Burger King drive-through. That said, would you become one of the walking undead, or would you choose to live out your natural life to its predestined conclusion, whatever that may be? Let's take a closer look at what you would be up against.

ONE IS A LONELY NUMBER

Both in literature and film, the aspect of vampires as lonely creatures is often emphasized, usually playing upon the fact that century upon century of stalking and hiding in the shadows slowly breeds a measure of insanity.

> As some vampires do, Anne Rice's preternaturals have the ability to disappear for centuries at a time, burying themselves for a prolonged rest until which time they reawaken and reassert their immortality.

In the *Underworld* films, the vampire elders "leapfrog through time," one ruling their coven a century at a time while the others sleep in a mummified state until reanimated via blood transfusions. There's a strong logic in those clever processes, as not only is the vampire re-energized by their extended nap, but once oriented to their current era, they're able to function—in most cases—with few hints of psychological impairment.

The bottom line for most vampires is that at one time or another most succumb to depression or madness as a result of realizing that as an undead predatorial species they are truly alone. Now that's not to say that there aren't contingents of blood fiends who have no remorse and no earthly qualms about wreaking havoc on humanity.

Most certainly these monsters are prevalent throughout fiction, film, and especially folklore, but the fact remains that no matter a vampire's level of aggression, the so-called dark gift of immortality is more often a curse that manifests itself in myriad ways, through violence, madness, depression, psychosis, or bloodthirsty revenge. All of that must be considered by those considering a vampiric transformation.

DO OR DIE

Here again is another point of consideration. If a vampire is to remain a vampire they have little choice in their survival: They must kill to survive or be killed for others' survival. This comes down to one basic factor—blood (see Chapter 3). The majority of vampires in folklore, fiction, and film feast on human blood, with a contingent of reluctant vamps choosing animal blood or synthetic blood for sustenance. Still others, like Blade (see Chapters 8 and 10) use injectables in order to control the thirst and forgo killing anything for the sole purpose of food. Yeah, it's cool. But it's also a movie.

Something else to ponder. In the television series *Forever Knight*, Nicholas de Brabant, otherwise known as homicide detective Nick Knight, drinks animal blood in an effort to make restitution for all the lives he's taken over eight centuries (see Chapter 11). That's not to say he doesn't occasionally succumb to his vampiric urges, because he does.

That issue plagues even the most hardcore reluctant vamps. They long to be human again and be rid of the madness that comes with stalking and destroying humans. Of course in the meantime, they have no choice but to obtain blood by any means possible, be it from a rat, a junkie, an heiress, or in some cases, another vampire or otherworldly creature such as a werewolf. So if you're thinking that being a vampire is the ultimate in coolness, bear in mind that the happy little picnic that is immortality comes with torrents of fire ants determined to stake a claim in your demise.

Tales from the Crypt

Vampires are nothing if not resourceful creatures whether it comes to ensnaring their prey, creating a coven, or just blending into society while at the same bleeding them dry without being detected. In Chapter 4 we discussed the origins of the vampire's coffin and the necessity of resting on native soil. If you're interested in living the lifestyle of the "vampyre," let's expand on the notion of how you would go about procuring and securing an abode fit for the undead.

FINDING NEW DIGS

Let's assume for a moment that you're a bloodsucker. Last night, one of Van Helsing's pesky descendants found your lair and set fire to it. You managed to save your ash, but now you need a new place to shack up. What do you do?

Well, the most logical and efficient means of securing a new domicile is to bite the hand that feeds you—literally—and then take over their residence. For the literary and celluloid vampire this is a common practice and a rather ingenious way of acquiring not only homeland security, but building up financial resources.

That is, assuming it's done correctly. Making Brad Pitt your Saturday night sushi combo and then moving into his place would obviously draw too much attention. No, the best avenue to take is to hunt down some reclusive billionaire whose holdings you can acquire by means of hypnosis, and posing as a family member, to build your assets from there.

Many modern-day fictional and celluloid vampires fluctuate between hanging out in spare quarters, constantly moving from place to place, or undertaking a sumptuous existence in a private mansion or castle. For the coven in the film *Underworld*, it is a mansion, and being the business-savvy suckers they are, they own Ziodex Industries which produces cloned blood. Who says a vampire can't make blood money, eh?

FLIGHT PLAN

Here's another thing to ponder. The most successful vampires always have an escape plan or devious mechanism by which they can avoid attacks or even capture. As we discussed in Chapter 3, the need for top-notch security is a must in regard to living arrangements. So too is the ability to adapt to any given situation, which for a vampire who has an aversion to daylight means finding the nearest dark place available. Awareness and agility in this case is crucial to vampiric survival. If you don't stay sharp as to the dawn's arrival, you could end up hiding in some remote Port-O-Potty. And nobody—dead or undead—wants *that*.

Preternatural Diet

Here's a biggie in your decision to become a demonic menace. Given the concept that "the blood is the life," a vampire's most obvious diet is, of course, blood. That could be the blood of humans, animals, synthetic blood, or a range of other odd blood-related concoctions. Unless you're a vampire of the reluctant nature who's prone to robbing blood banks, then the acquisition of blood generally requires your taking a life.

For the traditional vampire, a dietary plan is highly predictable and boring in regard to variety save for several blood types. That means no more Big Macs, Oreos, or Starbucks Mochachinos. For the vampires of folklore, diets range from blood to the flesh of both humans and corpses and a wide range of human organs, birth-related matter, and other nasties such as entrails.

If you're gonna be a true bloodsucker, know that you'll have to go with the flow. Oh, and for the record, as of this writing no one's come up with low-carb hemoglobin. It's all or nothing.

A Bloody Good Show

Okay. So now you've been introduced to the bare facts of what you'll face when becoming a vampire. Now it's time to get down to the most important factors in your decision-making process—the ultimate pros and cons you must acknowledge and accept before letting someone turn you into his or her Bloody Mary.

The Downside:

- **Brunch:** There's no getting around the fact that Sunday brunches with your buddies will be a thing of the past. All food-related gatherings will require your claiming that you're on a permanent fast, or that you've already had lunch at your day job working at a blood bank.
- **Animal Companions:** Save for bats and wolves, pets are inadvisable. If for some reason you're unable to get your fangs on some poor unsuspecting human, Fluffy may become an hors d'oeuvre.
- **Bikinis:** Unless you're a daywalker, that itsy-bitsy teeny-weeny designer swimsuit is gonna rot in your closet for all eternity. You'll also bid farewell to tanning salons, surfing, and your Hawaiian timeshare.
- **Italian Cuisine:** Sadly, most vampires do have an aversion to garlic, which means saying *arrivederci* to lasagna, pizza, spaghetti carbonara and bolognaise, and any other food item containing the dreaded stinking rose. On the positive side, you'll save on Listerine.
- **Coffins:** If you're the type of vampire who's relegated to being boxed in then you'd better get over your claustrophobia—and fast. If you're of the variety that can maintain a semi-normal human existence, then rest easy—you can keep your bed.

- **Vanity:** If you're one to stand in front of the mirror for hours doing your hair and makeup, forget it. The last time you see yourself as a human is the last time you'll ever see yourself. Period. So prior to your being indoctrinated into the undead, make sure you're not wearing sweats and bunny slippers.
- **Family:** Unless your entire family is comprised of vampires, prepare to sever all ties to parents, siblings, close and extended family, your favorite Uncle Joe, reunions, birthdays, holidays, and basically everyone you've ever known and every tradition you hold dear. Sending Christmas cards is inadvisable as your inevitable immortal enemies would love to play Bad Santa and suck your family dry.

The Upside:

- **Airports:** If you're a flying vampire, travel will be cheap, there'll be no waiting for hours at airport security, and you won't have to relinquish seven dollars for a pillow and blanket on JetBlue. You can also hypnotize ticket agents to obtain extra air miles.
- **Sunglasses:** Given that you'll likely be wearing them all the time and you could be quite wealthy, designer shades like Gucci and Chanel will be your best friend. The same goes for shoes and any other designer labels you adore.
- **Web Surfing:** The fact that you're an immortal means that you might possibly have enough time to peruse every single site on the Internet. Maybe. You may also have enough time to actually get through Tolstoy's *War and Peace*.
- **Aging:** Immortals don't age one iota from the day of their rebirth, so the need for designer anti-wrinkle creams, moisturizers, plastic surgery, and anything containing Botox is officially negated.
- **Politics:** There's absolutely no need to take sides or dwell on any political issue whatsoever. If you want to endorse a candidate or adversely discredit one, just hypnotize them to suit your evil purposes.

- **Medical Insurance:** A substantial savings for all vampires, as your self-healing abilities eliminate the need for HMOs and co-payments. Dental visits are easily acquired with a bit of hypnosis.

Given all of this vital information, the choice of becoming a vampire is entirely up to you. Choose wisely and know that whichever way you go, immortality, as with all epic temptations, can give you more than just heartburn. That said, it's time to switch gears and offer you a bit of advice in regard to vampire detection.

Is Your Neighbor a Nosferatu?

So you're sitting in your living room staring out the window at the house across the street. The huge exterior is decidedly overgrown and unkempt, the windows are covered with black paper, and there's a barbed wire security fence around the entire perimeter. You never see anyone or anything save for smoke wafting out of the chimney with vague regularity. But every so often, you think you catch a glimpse of a shadow moving around the yard. Is it a neighborhood cat, or is your neighbor a nosferatu?

HOW DO YOU SPOT A VAMPIRE?

Given their ability to meld into society, immortals can be tricky to identify. According to most experts, the one commonality among vampires is the pallor of their skin, which can range from white to grayish to greenish to translucent. Of course in the modern era, how does one distinguish a vampire from a Marilyn Manson fan? If you're determined to identify a vampire, there are several things to look for:

- **Their skin color.** As mentioned above, are they white as a sheet, or ghostlike in their appearance? If burned during a flambé accident, do they immediately regenerate? Also worthy of note are extremely red lips, which could indicate a recent feeding.

- **An aversion to garlic.** A fact that should preclude the possibility of ever finding a vampire hanging out at Pizza Hut or any Olive Garden restaurant. They may also have a reaction to wolfsbane, silver, hawthorn, or anything resembling a long sharply pointed object.
- **A dislike of or total aversion to holy artifacts including but not limited to crosses, crucifixes, Eucharist wafers, biblical passages, or holy water.** If touched by a religious icon, their skin may even burn. Take care though, as many modern bloodsuckers have absolutely no issue with holy icons.
- **Unlike humans, vampires will be icy cold to the touch.** Without a beating heart to send warm blood throughout their circulatory system they will be both literally and figuratively cold-hearted critters.
- **A lack of mirrors in their home or on their person, as well as a lack of reflection in a mirror.** Also, if your overly friendly neighbor's smiling face is missing from the group photos taken at your latest barbecue, it's likely *not* Kodak's fault.
- **The color black.** Any vampire worth their hemoglobin will dress entirely in black. But be warned—many a vampire will retain various adornments, commonly red, white, or silver in color, so as to maintain fashion and throw hunters off the scent. They may also wear sunglasses in the dead of night or wear clothes that were fashionable in the late twelfth century.
- **No shadow, or alternately, a shadow that moves independent of the vampire.** If your neighbor is dancing the conga and his shadow is sitting in the La-Z-Boy watching *Monday Night Football*, you've got a problem.
- **Abnormal canines.** And by this we don't mean mutant Labradors. A vampire's fangs may extend when they're ready to feed, but in their dormant position, the canines may appear a bit elongated or exceptionally sharp. If they can open a can without a can opener . . . be afraid.

- **The fact that they rise at dusk and remain awake until dawn, claiming that they're "night owls."** To test this, trying inviting them to Sunday brunch.
- **They may smell of freshly dug earth, indeed reeking of it like a cheap cologne.** If they're not a botanist or gravedigger by profession, a vampire could be afoot.
- **A consistent appearance.** Vampires are creatures of habit and obsession, whereby they may always look the same in regard to attire, but most especially in regard to aging. Their physical appearance, right down to the last wrinkle, will remain eternal. If you don't see a liver spot, be warned. Your liver may be in jeopardy.

Gypsies, Vamps, and Seas

Amid an ocean of lore, legend, fiction, and film, we've learned that there's always more to be gleaned by the study of vampires. While it's certain that this tale has by no means told all there is to tell about the ultimate immortal bad boys and girls, it's hoped that what has been revealed beneath the vampire's cloak entices you to further explore the genre. As a researcher and chronicler, I am like many other literary gypsies, who throughout history alternately hunt or are in league with these nightcrawlers. That is, of course in the metaphorical sense. As an appropriate exit into the eternal mist of darkness, it is *Dracula*'s Abraham Van Helsing who writes the final immortal words:

> *"All men are mad in some way or the other, and inasmuch as you deal discreetly with your madmen, so deal with God's madmen too, the rest of the world. You tell not your madmen what you do nor why you do it. You tell them not what you think. So you shall keep knowledge in its place, where it may rest, where it may gather its kind around it and breed."*

No matter your take on the vampire legend, I do behoove you to remember those sage words of wisdom the next time you run across an immortal bad boy. For to know a vampire is to appreciate their struggle, while at the same time keeping your inner Buffy well armed and at the ready the next time you see a gorgeous hunk emerge from the shadows and nuzzle your neck in a breathy embrace.

Appendix

Glossary

Alp: A German demon that attacks women in their sleep, causing nightmares and hysteria.

Alucard: The reverse spelling of *Dracula*, often taken as a name by various reincarnations of the character.

***Angel*:** A TV series spinoff of *Buffy the Vampire Slayer*, featuring the tall, handsome vampire, Angel, played by David Boreanaz.

Balderston, John L.: American screenwriter who adapted Hamilton Deane's version of *Dracula* for the theater, and who helped create the successful 1931 American film version.

***Baobban Sith*:** Seductive maidens who lure traveling men into frivolous partying, and then kill them in their sleep.

***Bhuta*:** Vampiric creatures of India who steal the bodies of the living and then feed on other humans.

Blade: A Marvel Comics character adapted for a film trilogy starring Wesley Snipes. Blade is a half-human, half-vampire who hunts vampires.

Blaylock, Miriam: An alien vampire who loses her human companions to the ravages of time in Whitley Strieber's 1981 novel, *The Hunger*, and the 1983 film. See ***Hunger, The***.

Blood: The oxygen-bearing liquid in humans that sustains life. Blood is also the source of life for most vampires.

Bride: A typical reference to female companions chosen by vampires.

Bringing Over: See **Crossing Over.**

***Buffy the Vampire Slayer*:** A 1992 film and long-running TV series featuring cheerleader turned vampire-hunter Buffy Summers.

Buffyverse: A term used to encompass all things Buffy-related, including the TV series, video games, and a huge collection of novels, graphic novels, fan sites, and paraphernalia.

***Camazotz*:** A South American demon with the body of a human and the head of a bat.

Carpathians: A mountain range running through much of eastern Europe, renowned for its mention in the novel *Dracula*.

Chelsea Quinn Yarbro: Author of the *St. Germain* series, and one of the most prolific writers and novelists for over thirty years.

Chupacabra: A creature in recent Mexican and southern American lore believed to attack livestock and drain their blood.

Cihuateteo: The souls of women who perish in childbirth, and who bring strength to warriors and death to travelers.

Cock's Crow: A term indicating the onset of dawn.

Coffin: A box in which corpses are buried. Often used as the resting place of vampires.

Consecrated Ground: Religious or blessed areas where vampires dare not tread.

Count Duckula: British cartoon spinoff of *Danger Mouse*, featuring a vegetarian vampire duck who dodged the vampire hunter Dr. Von Goosewing for sixty-five episodes in the late 1980s.

Count Orlock: The hideous rat-faced Dracula played by German actor Max Schreck in the 1922 film *Nosferatu*.

Count Von Count: Famed *Sesame Street* muppet who teaches toddlers how to count.

Cross: Any informal representation of a crucifix, often used with equal success against vampires.

Crossing Over: The process of becoming a vampire after being bitten by one.

Crossroads: A place where vampires are thought to gather together and attack travelers.

Crucifix: An effective vampire deterrent, representative of Jesus Christ on the cross on which he was crucified.

Cullen, Edward: Stephenie Meyer's hunky vampire and Bella's love interest in the *Twilight* series. See ***Twilight***.

Cushing, Peter: English actor, best known for his portrayals of Abraham Van Helsing. Cushing worked with Christopher Lee in over nineteen films.

Dark Shadows: A 1960s daytime television drama featuring vampire Barnabas Collins and the eerie doings at Collinwood estate. See **Frid, Jonathan**.

de Lioncourt, Lestat: The most renowned literary vampire since Dracula and protagonist of Anne Rice's legendary *Vampire Chronicles*.

de Pointe du Lac, Louis: Protagonist and reluctant vampiric partner of Lestat in Anne Rice's 1976 novel *Interview with the Vampire*.

Deane, Hamilton: English actor and playwright who created the first successful stage adaptation of Bram Stoker's *Dracula*.

Dracula: Bram Stoker's seminal 1897 novel which is the genesis for hundreds of future films and vampiric novels. It hasn't been out of print since its first publication.

Dracula: The legendary antagonistic vampire character of Bram Stoker's novel *Dracula*. The name also refers to the Wallachian ruler Prince Vlad Dracula.

Eucharist Wafer: The bread or cracker representation of the body of Jesus Christ in religious ceremonies. Often used to ward off vampires.

Forever Knight: A 1990s television series starring Geraint Wyn Davies as Nick Knight, a remorseful vampire intent on repaying his sins to society.

Frid, Jonathan: Canadian actor who played vampire Barnabas Collins on the gothic soap opera *Dark Shadows*.

Garlic: An ancient bulb vegetable used for food and flavoring, and as a pungent deterrent to vampires.

Gwrach y Rhibyn: A hideously aged female creature in England and Wales who attacks children and drains their blood to cause illness and death.

Hammer Films: The prolific producer of *Dracula* and other vampire films during the 1950s, 60s and 70s.

Harker, Jonathan: One of the primary heroes of Bram Stoker's *Dracula*. Fiancé of Mina Murray.

Highgate Cemetery: A London cemetery where an infamous vampire hunt took place in the 1970s.

Holmwood, Arthur: Lucy Westenra's fiancé in Bram Stoker's novel, *Dracula*.

Holy Water: Water blessed by priests for religious services. It is used to burn the skin of vampires.

***Hunger, The*:** One of author Whitley Strieber's most famous novels, published in 1981. Also a 1983 film starring Catherine Deneuve. See **Blaylock, Miriam**.

Hypnotism: The process of inducing a state of consciousness during which a person becomes responsive to suggestion. A favorite technique of vampires for claiming victims.

***Interview with the Vampire*:** Anne Rice's first book in *The Vampire Chronicles*. *Interview* relates the story of vampire Louis de Pointe du Lac and his maker, Lestat de Lioncourt.

***Jiang Shi*:** A Chinese "hopping ghost" thought to be the reanimated corpse of a drowning, suicide, or hanging victim that attacks and kills humans.

***Kappa*:** A monkey-like Japanese critter that springs from waterways to attack humans.

***Lamia*:** A Libyan princess in Greek mythology who bore the wrath of Zeus' jealous wife, Hera, and took revenge on humans.

***Lamiai*:** Incarnations of the mythological Lamia who suck blood from children and seduce young men into their own ruin.

***Lampir*:** A Bosnian vampire that crawls from the grave to spread sickness and death.

Langella, Frank: American actor who played Dracula onstage and in the 1979 made-for-television version.

***Langsuyar*:** Vampires who spring from the bodies of a mother and child who perish during childbirth. The mother becomes a *langsuyar*, and the child becomes a *pontianak*.

Le Fanu, Sheridan: Author of the 1872 novella "Carmilla," featuring the first female vampire.

Lee, Christopher: English actor who's been in over 260 films, and who played Dracula over seventeen times.

Lugosi, Bela: Hungarian actor who played Dracula in the American stage production, and 1931 film, *Dracula* among others.

Lycan: Modern variation of the term *lycanthrope*, used to describe werewolves. See **Werewolf**.

Lycanthrope: A werewolf. See **Werewolf**.

Maker: A vampire who creates another vampire from one of its victims.

Mesmerism: See **Hypnotism**.

Meyer, Stephenie: Author of the *Twilight* series of young adult vampire novels. See *Twilight*.

Mirror: An object thought to irritate vampires because they can cast no reflection in them.

Morris, Quincey P.: The sole American in Bram Stoker's *Dracula*. Morris is responsible for issuing the final blow that kills Dracula.

Munsters, The: A 1960s situation comedy featuring characterizations of vampires, werewolves, and Frankenstein's monster.

Murray, Mina: Dracula's primary obsession and surviving victim in Bram Stoker's *Dracula*.

Nachtzeherer: A German vampire that returns from the dead after tearing at its hands and limbs with its teeth.

Native Soil: The ground in which a vampire was laid to rest before returning from the dead.

Nosferatu: A Symphony of Horror: The 1922 classic silent film starring Max Schreck as Count Orlock in an unauthorized interpretation of Bram Stoker's *Dracula*.

Nosferatu: A "carrier of disease." Stoker incorrectly used the term to define vampires, and the term is now entrenched in vampire lore.

Oldman, Gary: English actor who played Dracula in the blockbuster 1992 film, *Bram Stoker's Dracula*.

Paole, Arnod: A former Serbian soldier turned "real-life" vampire who's responsible for creating the Medvegia Vampires in the late 1720s.

Penanggala: An Indonesian vampire that assumes the shape of a severed head with entrails dangling from its neck.

Penny Dreadful: Cheap storybooks printed in England during the 1800s.

Plogojowitz, Peter: A Serbian peasant who died in 1725, and is one of the most famous "real-life" vampires.

Poenari Castle: A fortified stronghold in Romania thought to be the only "castle" of the real Vlad Dracula.

Polidori, John: Author of *The Vampyre*, published in 1819, which featured Lord Ruthven. See *Vampyre, The*.

Pontianak: See **Langsuyar**.

Preternatural: Creatures or experiences beyond what is natural.

Rakshasas: Fanged Indonesian ogre-like vampires that attack pregnant women and infants.

Reanimation: The return to life after death.

Renfield, R.M.: The lunatic in Dr. Seward's asylum who eventually helps bring about the fiend's demise in the novel, *Dracula*.

Revenant: A person who has returned from the dead.

Rice, Anne: Renowned author of the *Vampire Chronicles*, who triggered a booming and continued interest in vampires starting in 1976 with *Interview with the Vampire*.

Salem's Lot: The second novel of horror icon Stephen King, which depicts what might have happened if Dracula came to a small town in Maine during the twentieth century.

Salt: The oldest food additive known to mankind, and often used to repel vampires.

Schrattl: A variation of the German alp that attacks livestock and drives humans to insanity.

Schreck, Max: See **Count Orlock**.

Seeds: Often spread on pathways to distract vampires, who are thought to have to count them one by one.

Seward, Dr. Jack: The owner of an English lunatic asylum in England. One of the heroes of Bram Stoker's *Dracula* and former pupil of Abraham Van Helsing.

Southern Vampires: A series created by author Charlaine Harris featuring Sookie Stackhouse and her escapades in a Louisiana town inhabited by newly legalized vampires, humans, and other preternatural creatures.

St. Germain, Count of: Chelsea Quinn Yarbro's legendary vampire featured in a twenty-book series that began in the late 1970s and continues to this day.

Stake: Sharpened wooden or metal spikes used for driving into revenants or vampires, which typically causes immediate death.

Stoker, Bram: Author of the 1897 novel *Dracula*.

Striga: An Albanian witch that transforms into a flying insect at night to suck the blood from the living.

Strigoi Mort: See *Strigoi*.

Strigoi Vii: See *Strigoi*.

Strigoi: A Romanian revenant, thought to leave its grave and take the form of an animal to harass humans. The *strigoi vii* was a witch who would become a vampire after death. The *strigoi mort* was the vampire after death.

Swan, Bella: Stephenie Meyer's female protagonist in the young adult *Twilight* series. See *Twilight*.

Tlahuelpuchi: A bloodsucking South American witch who attacks infants.

Transylvania: The central Romanian setting used as Dracula's homeland in Bram Stoker's 1897 novel *Dracula*.

True Blood: An HBO television series based on author Charlaine Harris's Sookie Stackhouse/*Southern Vampire* series. See *Southern Vampires*.

Twilight: Stephenie Meyer's young adult vampire series featuring Bella Swan and Edward Cullen. Also a 2008 motion picture.

Upir: A Slovakian revenant thought to spread disease, and one that can kill with a glance from its evil eye.

Uppyr: A Russian vampire believed to be the undead remains of a religious heretic.

Ustrel: A Bulgarian spirit created from the souls of unbaptized children born on Saturdays. Ustrels hide between the horns and legs of livestock and drain their blood.

Vampir: A Bulgarian vampire that returned from the dead as a human of healthy appearance. It behaves normally by day, and harasses the living by night.

Vampire Bat: A South American bat that subsists on the blood of mammals and birds.

Vampire Chronicles, The: Anne Rice's enormously successful series of books that created the foundation for generations of vampire novels and novelists.

Vampire: A corpse returned from the dead to harass and often drink the blood of the living.

Vampirologist: A person dedicated to the study, and often destruction, of vampires.

Vampyre, The: A story by John Polidori from the early 1800s that featured the vampire Lord Ruthven. The story helped set the stage for Bram Stoker's *Dracula*.

Van Helsing, Abraham: The fictional Dutch scholar, intellectual, and vampirologist who is the hero of Stoker's novel *Dracula*. He is the father of all vampire hunters.

Varney, Sir Francis: The lead character in *Varney the Vampyre*. See *Varney the Vampyre*.

Varney the Vampyre: An English penny dreadful series of 109 stories written in the mid-1840s by James Malcolm Rymer that featured a reanimated corpse that stalked young girls.

Vetala: A spirit in Hindu mythology that takes possession of corpses.

Vlad Dracula: The fourteenth-century ruler of Wallachia who became infamous for impaling his enemies on poles and famous in Romania as a national hero. Vlad Dracula was the inspiration for the name of Bram Stoker's title character in the novel *Dracula*.

Vlad Tepes: See **Vlad Dracula**.

Vlad the Impaler: See **Vlad Dracula**.

Vrykolakas: Creatures who return from the dead and become demons that causes disease and misfortune among humans.

Welsh *Hag*: A female demon in Wales who can take the form of a young woman, a matron, or an old crone to bring misfortune and death to any who see her.

Werewolf: A human who transforms into a wolf or wolf-like creature during certain time periods, generally associated with the full moon.

Westenra, Lucy: One of Dracula's victims in Bram Stoker's novel. Lucy was transformed into a vampire and staked to death by her fiancé, Arthur Holmwood.

Woodwives: German fairies who have a peaceful appearance, but who attack and kill travelers, woodcutters, and hunters who invade their forest habitat.